TOUR OF LOVE

Lighthouse Lovers
Book 1

SHANNON O'CONNOR

Content Warnings

Please note some of these might be considered spoilers for parts of the story.
- Eating disorders including Anorexia
(discussed on page; FMC is in recovery for last 10+ years)
- Grief/Loss of parent
(Past, off page but discussed on page)
- Cheating
(Past, off page but discussed on page)
(Not between main characters)
- Loss of a loved one
(Not main characters; distant side character)

Body Like A Back Road - Sam Hunt

Hands to Myself - Selena Gomez

talk me out of it - Olivia Holt

Stranger - Riley Roth

Crush - Tessa Violet

I Really Like You - Carly Rae Jepsen

Sucker - Jonas Brothers

Espresso - Sabrina Carpenter

Starving - Hailee Steinfeld, Grey, Zedd

Slow Hands - Niall Horan

Toothbrush - DNCE

I Think I'm In Love - Kat Dahlia

ONE

Heather

"**A**re you sure your parents won't mind me staying here?" I ask Alana one last time over the phone. I'm pulling into the cul-de-sac of her family's property, this is her last chance to change her mind.

"Yes. They're happy you're visiting, and besides, it's not like we even use them. I'm not sure why we even own five houses on the property. It's very unnecessary, if you ask me." Alana brushes me off, and I know I shouldn't worry. She's one of my best and oldest friends; she wouldn't have offered if it wasn't a genuine offer.

"Okay, I'm pulling up now. The key is in the mailbox, right?" I ask.

"Yep, let me go. I have to go with Will to pick out his tux. If I leave it to him, he'll be marrying me in a bright-blue suit." She sighs.

"Good luck!" She hangs up and I turn toward the house. It's even bigger than I remember.

Alana's family is rich, which is something we always knew growing up, but when they bought this property with five summer homes on the coast of Lovers, Maine we realized just how rich they are. Alana and I—along with Ryleigh, Norah, and Kim—have been inseparable for the last ten years, even though we grew apart as we went to separate colleges and started our lives. We never lost touch, and we're all coming together again for Alana's wedding at the end of the summer.

I pull up to the mailbox at the end of the driveway and park for a second. After grabbing the key from the mailbox, I jump back into my car and head up the driveway. The house is comparable to the one Noah built Allie in *the Notebook*. A big, beautiful wraparound porch. Light pink paint that covers the house with huge windows throughout. A magnificent front yard that seems to go on for miles. Although I can see Alana's family's other homes on the property, there's no way to get to them without driving. My favorite part is how this specific house overlooks the water—oh! And I can see the Lovers Lighthouse from here. It's my favorite place in the town; it brings me a sense of peace just being able to see it from here.

After stopping to take it all in, I walk up the front steps and unlock the front door. It smells like lemon-scented cleanser, which I'm sure is the work of Alana's parents' housekeeper. I assured them they didn't need to pull out any fancy stops for me, after all, I've been living in a one-bedroom in Vermont for the last few years. But it's just like Alana to not listen to me anyway.

I open up a few of the windows in the living room and kitchen to air out the smell and start unloading my car. I only have a few boxes and two suitcases. Not that this is all my stuff, but I shipped most of my stuff to my parents' when I knew I was moving back to town. They have the space to hold everything for me while I stay here and look for a new apartment in town.

"Hellllooooo?!" I hear a voice chime from the living room. I drop the box I'm carrying on the kitchen island and run to them.

"May!" I pick up my baby sister and swing her around.

"HJ!" She giggles and rolls her eyes as I put her down.

"It's been way too long." I smile. Taking her in, I realize how crazy it is to refer to her as my baby sister. I saw her a few months ago, but she's almost twenty-four now, and she's lost that child-like look about her.

"I know, you finally come home now that I'm moving out of

state," May adds sheepishly, clearly trying to drop a bomb on me like it was nothing.

"What?!" I exclaim.

"Yeah, I, uh. I'm moving to New York next week. I was waiting to tell you in person," she says, rubbing the back of her neck while my eyes widen.

"New York!? Have you even visited before?" I ask, confused.

"Well, no. But my girlfriend is sort of from there, and we think we'll have better job opportunities there. It's a career move for us." May pushes her dirty blonde hair out of her face, and I search it for any hint that I should be worried she's moving far away. But all I see is a new calmness about her.

"The girlfriend you used to compete with in high school for solos?" I raise an eyebrow. Her and Clara had been sworn enemies for the four years they were in school together. They were the best dancers in town, always competing for the lead spot in any dance competition.

"Technically, yes. But we, uh, don't fight anymore. She's really amazing." She blushes. It was a tad surprising when my sister called me up a few months ago and told me she was dating a woman. Not for the reasons one would think, but because now my parents have ended up with two queer kids. Not that they mind in the slightest, we're lucky in that department.

"I hope you'll bring her around for dinner or something before you leave." I smile.

"Of course, now should I help with the last of the boxes?"

"Yes, please." I nod.

We head out to the car, grab the last of my stuff, pile it in the front entryway, and head to the kitchen. If I know my best friend, the kitchen is be fully stocked even though I assured her that wasn't necessary. Sure enough, when I open the cabinets and fridge, they're stocked with my favorite snacks and treats. I pull out a bag of sweet potato chips, two bowls, and pour some for May and I.

"So, why aren't you just moving in with mom and dad? Like, they have the room…" May says, crunching a chip.

"I just want to be alone right now while I figure out my next step. I'm apartment hunting this summer, picking up some photographing jobs and helping Alana with wedding preparations," I explain.

"I guess that makes sense." She shrugs.

"I'm happy for you, you know. That you're moving to New York to follow your dreams. It's just a little surprising." I don't have to explain further, she knows what I mean. May has always been very type-A about everything, so picking up and leaving our hometown is a bit out of character for her.

"I know. I just think I need to make a change like this. Clara pushes me to be a bit more carefree, and I'm thankful for that." She smiles.

"I can tell; you seem calmer in general. It's almost like your aura took a chill pill or something," I tease.

"Oh shush." She rolls her eyes.

"So are you staying over tonight? Sister sleepover before we're in different states again?" I ask hopefully.

"That sounds great. But I'm going to need more than just some chips." She laughs.

"Yes, I've had a craving for a vegan burger from Teddy's for months now," I say, rubbing my stomach.

"Yes, please! Well, a real burger for me. But I haven't been to Teddy's in forever."

"Let me change into something else and then we can go." I grab one of my suitcases and head toward the bedrooms. There are four total, so I pick the closest one to the living room and claim it as my own.

I'll unpack more later, but for now, I throw some of my clothes around and look for something cute to wear. Lovers is a small town, and you never know who you might run into. So, I like to always dress to impress—just in case. I twirl my light-pink hair into a braid, ignoring my blonde roots growing out. I'll need a touch up sooner than later, but that'll have to wait. For now, I grab a pair of white cotton shorts and a floral tank top. I look in the mirror quickly to brush a splash of makeup on my face, and then I head back to May.

At the last moment, I reach into one of the boxes and grab my camera.

"Really?" She sighs and I nod. I don't like to go anywhere without it.

We take her car since it was parked behind mine, and we head into town. It had been months since I've been home, so it's nice seeing everything again. Especially in the summer—that's my favorite season to spend here. May talks about Clara, their upcoming move, and lets me scroll through her phone to look at photos of their apartment. They found a place close to the agency they were using to find jobs and already have two auditions lined up. I'm a proud big sister in this moment. From watching May go from twirling around our room to growing up to a professional dancer…it's a big moment.

We get to Teddy's, and I'm happy to say it hasn't changed. The bar and grill look the same as always. The old signs and art hanging on the walls brings me back to my childhood. It's dark inside— despite it still being light out—and the booths are still tearing at the seams. It's refreshing to see some things never change. I notice Wrenn, Alana's younger sister, behind the bar. She waves over at us. She was always tagging around with us when we were younger, never quite part of the group. Now we're older, and from what Alana's told me, they are quite a bit closer than they used to be. We take a seat at one of the booths, grabbing the menus on the left of the table, and we look them over despite knowing what we want.

"Know what you want?" a guy who can't be older than twenty-one asks.

"Yes please. The vegan burger, a side salad, and an iced tea," I say.

"Dressing?"

"Balsamic?" I ask hopefully. It's hard getting a salad when you're out as a vegan. Most of the dressings have things I can't have.

"Sure." He writes it down and then turns to May.

"The All-American bacon cheeseburger with onion rings and a vanilla milkshake." She smiles.

He nods and walks away to put in our order. I've never seen May order so much food, but I'd never say that out loud. She knows her body, who cares what she orders?

"I have been craving a burger this week. And I've been doing double workouts to train for this audition," she says, slurping her milkshake.

"You have amazing dedication," I say admiringly.

"I just hope it'll pay off in New York. It's almost like starting over."

"Yeah, but you pay your dues and it'll be worth it," I assure her.

"I hope so. Do you have any gigs lined up since you're back?"

"I have a wedding coming up, actually. The couple is super nice so I'm looking forward to it." I love shooting weddings. There's just something about the happiness and joy that comes out of such a fun day.

"Have you run into Jane yet?" She looks at me curiously, and I sigh, I knew this might come up.

"Nope." I grind my teeth. The mention of my ex tends to do that. I know there's a chance I might run into her eventually; it *is* a small town, after all. What I dread the most is knowing she'll be at Alana's wedding with her shiny new girlfriend on her arm—the same one who she cheated on me with—while I'll be showing up to the wedding stag. I'm better off without her, but I don't want it to look like she's *winning* the breakup. Yeah, yeah. I shouldn't care about things like that, but I can't help it. When someone fucks you over the way she did to me, sometimes you can't help but care about what they think.

Sage

___

"Are you still doing that practice test?" Maeve asks, walking back from the bathroom. Her bouncy blonde curls are tied back with a clip, which means she's in focus mode. We both have a huge psychology exam we need to pass in order to stay in the class.

"I did it twice already. I'm doing it again," I admit.

"What did you get the first two times?" she asks, taking a seat.

"Uh, a ninety-nine and a ninety-eight," I say sheepishly.

Her mouth drops open. "Are you serious?! Then why are you retaking it?"

"I just want to be sure that it wasn't a fluke."

"Once is a fluke, twice means you know the material," she insists.

"I'm almost done, then we can work on the essay part of our project," I tell her.

"Okay, I'll work on my biology homework while you finish up," she says, shaking her head.

Maeve and I were paired up on the first day of freshman year when we were just babies in English 101. Neither of us even knew where the cafeteria even was back then. We got along right away, and as it turned out, we were both social work majors. It put us in a lot of the same classes over the years, and for a while, we even became roommates. That was back when I lived on campus, though. Now I'm in the grad program with her, and we both live in town. I miss being her roommate, but I also enjoy having an apartment to myself.

I refocus on my exam, reading over the multiple choice questions again to make sure it wasn't a trick question. That was what got me a ninety-eight the first time. I'm sure Maeve was right, and I don't *need* the practice, but I also can't afford to fail this class and lose my scholarship. I need to be sure that I know the material so I keep my 4.0 GPA. There's no wiggle room in the scholarship. If I don't maintain the perfect GPA, they'll discontinue the money. Something that's keeping me afloat. No way would I be able to keep paying school on a tour guide's salary.

Clicking the answers on the screen in front of me, the score 100 pops up, and I let a small breath out. At least I can relax now. I pull up our essay notes and look at Maeve.

"Okay, ready?" I smile.

"Yes, so I was thinking we'd talk about the statistics of the foster care system, then lead into why that number is so high compared to adoption rates."

"Okay." I start typing away, making notes and highlighting where we should add certain data.

"What do you think of her?" Maeve points her pencil not-so-obviously behind me, and I turn around slightly to see the brunette she's pointing at.

"She's cute." I shrug then turn back to the essay.

"So why don't you ask her out?" She purses her lips.

"What?" I frown.

"Why don't you ask her out?" she repeats.

"Uh, because we're in the middle of working on an essay?"

"You know what I mean. You never go out anymore, you should ask someone out before your life passes you by." Maeve sighs.

"You know I don't have time to date. I'm here studying, at the lighthouse working, or sleeping. When would I have time to date?"

"Well maybe if you cut back just a tiny bit on something, you'd have time to go out." She smiles.

"When I graduate I can date, for now it's just not in the plan," I say firmly. We've had this conversation before, but I know she means well. She's just worried about me. I haven't been out with anyone in a little over a year. Macey Dugan broke my heart by sleeping with three guys at once. I don't care what you want to do, but don't do it while you're someone's committed girlfriend.

"Then excuse me," Maeve fixes her shirt to expose the slightest bit more cleavage, and I smirk at my friend.

"Go for it." I laugh. Maeve is bold and beautiful, not to mention funny, so I'm sure she'll come back with a date for Saturday night.

I go back to looking at the essay notes when my phone buzzes on the table. My co-worker, Maren, texted me and asked if I can stay late tomorrow to cover someone else's call out. I check my schedule, thankful one of my classes had been cancelled and I actually could. My schedule is usually tight with work and classes, so I don't usually have the opportunity to say yes to overtime. I shoot off a quick reply, and then look back at the notes. I add in a few points that I want to make, and Maeve comes back with a proud smile on her face.

"You got it?" I guess.

"Oh, yes. Her name is Erica and we're going out on Friday night," she says, waving the Post-it in my face.

"Congrats." I roll my eyes.

"She might have a friend if you wanted to double…" She lets her voice trail.

"No thank you." I shake my head.

"Fine, but don't say I never tried." She shrugs. Maeve pops a piece of gum on her tongue and turns the computer toward her so she can see all the things I've added. She nods and starts typing a few things that I hadn't thought of.

"Shit, I have to grab dinner before my ethics class," I say looking at the time.

"Okay, I'll see you tomorrow. Don't stress about the test, you're going to do great." Maeve smiles.

"Thanks, don't have too much fun without me." I smirk and pack up my things.

The cafeteria was across campus but my class was in the building right next door. So I have just enough time to grab a sandwich from the deli, eat it, and then head to class. I glance at my Apple watch and check the time again, just to be sure. Yeah, I'm fine on time. I decide to grab a bag of chips and an apple since this class has a tendency to run late, and I'm always starving after. Picking a spot on the empty side of the cafeteria, I glance over my homework and fill in a few answers. I still have a few more days to turn it in, but I don't want to forget about it. I like getting it done the day I get it, that way there's not much of a chance that it'll slip my mind.

I'm not really friends with anyone in this class, so I sit in the front and keep to myself. I'm an old school notetaker, but my vision isn't really the best so I like to make sure I can see the board. I really should get some new glasses, but they weren't *that* old, and it's also an added cost I just can't afford have right now. The professor talks a little faster than I prefer, but I manage to note down everything she says. By the end of class, my hand is cramping and I'm ready to head home. It's my last class of the day, and I'll be at the lighthouse for tours bright and early tomorrow.

I drive from campus back to my apartment in Lovers, which is just a short fifteen-minute drive. Snacking on the potato chips on the way home, it curbs my appetite until I grab one of my meal-prepped meals. Tonight's meal is salmon, rice, and mixed vegetables. I set it in the microwave and turn on the television while I wait for it to heat up. I put on *Friends* just happy to have something on in the background while I eat. I don't have it in me to pay attention to anything with a storyline at this point. My food beeps, and I grab it from the microwave, take a spot on the couch, and press *play*.

Maybe Maeve was right; I do need to get out there again. It's been awhile, and I can afford a little leeway with my social life. When was the last time I did something that wasn't just work, school, or something for work or school? I'm embarrassed at the fact that it's been too long for me to even remember. I'm not going to just do some random blind date with Maeve's date, though. If I'm going to put myself out there, I want it to be authentic. Then again, how many queer women do I even come across in Maine? Not that many, honestly, and it isn't like relationships are knocking on my door.

Sighing, I clean up my plate from dinner and head to bed. Maybe I'll ease into things by hanging out with Maeve and her friends on a Saturday night or something. It isn't like I'm going to step outside and meet the love of my life now that I'm allowing myself a social life. I'm sure I have time.

THREE

Heather

My sister leaves before I wake because she has a mandatory—self-imposed—dance practice with Clara. So when I wake in the morning, I decide to unpack the stuff I brought in an attempt at moving in. I'm mostly just putting clothes in the closet and oversized dresser. While going through things, I find the box of pink hair dye and decide it's time to touch up my roots. Heading to the bathroom, I prep my hair and use the dye on the roots. I add a bit more than necessary just to make sure I don't miss any spots. While I'm waiting for the dye to settle in, I scroll on my phone for a bit. I *like* a few photos on Instagram, watch some videos on TikTok, and skip through some stories on Snapchat. I don't know why I even bother with social media anymore, nine out of ten times I don't see anything worth liking, but it's like checking the news. Just something to do to pass the time when I'm bored. Besides, how else would I get to see funny videos my friends send me?

The timer rings, and I hop in the shower to rinse out the hair dye. I remembered to put all my bath products in the bathroom during my unpacking session, so I use my special shampoo and strawberry body soap. I shave my legs, because I'm planning to wear shorts today. Wrapping a thick, fuzzy towel around me, I step out of the shower and head to my room. I look at my clothes but then sit on the edge of the bed and fall back into the satin sheets.

Eventually, I get dressed and meander into the kitchen to grab some breakfast. I'm glad Alana remembered I'm a vegan and prepared the fridge and cabinets with a lot of plant-based products. I fix myself a bowl of Cheerios with oat milk and sit on the island stool, looking out the window. The view is beautiful. I glance at the lighthouse in the distance and check the time on the oven. Maybe I should head to the lighthouse for a tour today. I don't have anything planned, and I would love to get some shots in. I can't remember the last time I took photos of it. Not that it changes much, but I like getting different boats or people or animals in the background.

After finishing breakfast, I'm grabbing my camera when an idea hits me. It takes me a little while to find them, but after looking in the last box I have, I find my business cards. I place a stack in my pocket before heading out to the lighthouse. It's not too crowded, but it is a Thursday and just past two in the afternoon. I lock my car, slip my keys in my pocket, and head inside. There's a small attachment to the lighthouse that acts as a museum and where you buy tickets for the tour. I wait my turn in line and glance up at the ceiling, taking in all the old relics.

"Next!" a voice calls, and I realize they're talking to me.

"Hi, sorry. I just need one ticket for the lighthouse, please," I say with a smile. I glance at their name tag. *Sage.* She's kind of hot. She has large, black-rimmed glasses, deep brown eyes, and a cute little dimple on her right cheek just above her chin.

"Okay, it'll be five-fifty. And just to let you know, you're welcome to take photos throughout the lighthouse and museum but there is currently no entry to the top of the lighthouse," Sage explains. Of course I already knew those things, but I nod anyway.

Handing Sage the money for the ticket, our hands touch lightly, and I blush. She hands me my change and a ticket. "You can head straight into the museum or to the left for the lighthouse." She points with a smile.

"Thank you," I say, and then I head into the museum to look

around first. Every so often, they get new pieces to put on display or new things to share. I take note of the new anchor they have and the history behind it. I grab a few quick photos of it and then head to the lighthouse entrance.

There's a family in front of me taking their time with the stairs, so I decide to hang back a bit and look around the bottom floor. I don't want to be rushed or stuck behind them.

"That was founded in 1903 by a family that still is native to Lovers," a voice quietly says behind me.

"What?" I turn back to see Sage glancing up at the framed piece of yellow map.

"Sorry, just giving you some history on the piece." She shrugs.

"Oh, thank you. I love learning about this place." I don't mention I've been coming here since I was old enough to walk here.

"I can tell you more if you like. I don't have a tour for a bit," she says, glancing at her Apple watch.

"Sure." I nod. *Is she flirting with me? Nah, she's just being kind and doing her job. I shouldn't think it's anything more than it is.* "I'm Heather," I extend a hand.

"I'm Sage." She smiles and shakes mine lightly.

"So, this piece was founded when the owners first bought the place back in 1901." She points at a piece of a boat that is encased in glass. "Most thought it was a part of an owner's boat, but it was supposedly pirates who sailed this boat."

"Really?" I ask, surprised. I never heard that before.

"Yeah, my boss doesn't like that note but I've seen the facts." She winks. Her eyelashes are thick and dark, matching her dark-black cropped hair. Her hair is similar to a Kristen Stewart crop.

"Is there a lot of stuff you know that isn't on the plaques?" I ask, raising an eyebrow.

"Oh, of course. That's why we always recommend taking a tour," she says proudly.

"Makes sense. I guess you'll have to slip me those secrets, then."

"Only if you promise not to tell." She smirks.

"Sure." I nod. The way she's looking at me makes me think there's something going on here, but that couldn't be, could it?

Sage leads me up the stairs to the entrance of the lighthouse. The spiral staircase opens up to a first floor that consists of an old kitchen. Sage starts to ramble on about the history of the kitchen, who first used it, who invented these specific models, and what they cooked. I know most of this, so I'm only half listening, but I pick my camera up off my shoulder and begin to snap some shots. Sage keeps talking while I snap away. I'm mostly grabbing purposeful, zoomed shots in order to get specific details. But then Sage's muscular and tattooed arm falls into the shot. She has a vine of roses on her tan skin. I snap a few photos, but then I discreetly point the camera at Sage, pretending I'm getting the art next to her. She steps slightly out of the way, and I grab her sharp jawline and dark eye as her hands are raised to explain her point. I can't help but admire not only her beauty but the passion when she speaks.

"Do you mind if I take some photos of you? I'm a photographer."

"You want photos of me?" she asks, surprised.

"Well, yeah? I usually edit them for my Instagram, but I'm also a professional photographer, so I take photos for websites and things, too."

"Oh, wait…edit how? Like you'll give me a mustache or something?" she teases.

"No, I probably wouldn't even have to do anything except mess with the lighting in here," I admit looking around.

"Okay, that's fine then." She shrugs, but I can tell how nervous she is now that she knows the camera is on her.

"Just go back to tour guide duties," I instruct. She nods and once she starts talking about the architecture of this building, the stress dissipates from her shoulders.

She leads me up the next flight of stairs to a room that they've staged as a bedroom. It's obvious that's what it once was, and they try to make it as authentic as possible. Sage talks about the daily life of a lighthouse keeper and the daily tasks they did. As she talks, I grab candid shots of her. She looks beautiful in every pose.

I'm happy to keep going until she glances at her watch and frowns.

"I have a tour in a few minutes. I'm sorry. I have to make sure they get the full tour."

"No worries, thanks for the insider info." I wink. Sage laughs and heads downstairs as I venture up the last flight of stairs. It's the bathroom for the lighthouse, which isn't too exciting to shoot. Instead of heading to the museum, I head to the dock outside the lighthouse.

It's early June, so it's nice and warm on the dock. The water is warm from the hot, glistening sun. I take some shots and then slip off my converse, place them on the side of me, and sit down on the edge of the dock. Looking out at the water with it crashing lightly at my feet, I feel a light peace wash over me. This is the only place I've ever felt at true peace. I'm safe from my thoughts here, and I'm able to control my overthinking and constant worrying. I know it'll all eventually work out, but the unknown haunts me. Will I find somewhere to live in town? Will I run into Jane while I'm here? Will I find a date to the wedding? All of those worries fade away when I sit on the edge of this dock.

I close my eyes for just a bit, taking in the blazing sun on my skin. Although I know I probably shouldn't, I burn too easily to properly enjoy it. The seagulls sound, and my eyes shoot open. Grabbing my camera, I take some photos of them over the water with a few boats in the background. Then, I stand to take some photos of the lighthouse with the town in the background. I don't know how long I'm out here, but it feels like hours. Eventually, someone from inside informs me that they're closing in a few minutes. I put my hand in my pocket and remember the business cards I want to give them. I know some people have weddings here, so I figured I'd ask the manager if they wouldn't mind keeping my card on file in case a couple needs a photographer.

"Hey, would I be able to speak to a manager?" I ask a young guy. His eyes widen. "Don't worry, it's nothing bad."

"Oh, then yeah, it's the girl over there." He points to Sage's back, and I smile. Hopefully this will go easier than planned.

"Hi, Sage? I was wondering if I could ask a question. The guy over there said you're the manager?" I smile tapping on her shoulder.

"Who..?" She glances at the guy I'm pointing to, and she nods, understanding. "I'm not the manager, but it's Todd's first day."

"Oh, I was hoping to talk to the manager. I just had a quick question. Are they here?"

"No, but what's your question?" she asks curiously.

"I was hoping I could leave some business cards here, and if any couples need a photographer for a wedding or any other event, you could give them the card?" I pull out the stack and hand one to Sage.

"We can definitely do that. I'll add them to the wedding paperwork we keep. Are you local?" she asks, looking at my card.

"Yeah, I'm staying at the Lover's Estate for the summer and then hopefully moving back. I'm here for my best friend's wedding at the end of the summer," I explain.

"Ah, okay." She nods.

"Thank you, and if you follow me on Instagram, I'll make sure to send you some of the photos of you." I smile.

"Instagram. Cool." She slides a card down the front of her khakis, and I smile again. Hopefully that means I might be hearing from her again.

FOUR

Sage

I'm flicking the paper between my fingers, staring down at the dark card. I know Heather said I could, but I'm a nervous wreck over the idea of following a woman on Instagram. It isn't like it means anything, she just wants to share some photos of me. Yet, here I am overthinking it. I can't help it, she's the most gorgeous woman I've seen in a long time. She said she was local to Lovers, but I've never seen her before. Not that I know everyone in town, but it isn't *that* big of a town. I shake my head and slide the card into the front of my jeans. I bend down to cuff them on the ends and slide on my Van's. My green Lighthouse Lovers Tours shirt is on with the sleeves also cuffed to show off my arm tattoos. What's the point of having tattoos if I can't show them off?

I grab a power bar and an iced coffee on my way to work and park in my usual employee spot at the end of the lot. It takes three minutes to get from my car to the clock in area, so I allow five just in case I need it. Sometimes that machine likes to give me a hard time about accepting my punch in numbers. But thankfully, today it was in a good mood.

I look over the schedule for the day while I sip my iced coffee, alternating between sipping and taking bites of my power bar. Two tour groups and three pre-paid tickets. This is a normal day for us.

We'll probably have ten visitors at most by the end of the day, and with any luck, we'll be out of here on time. I passed the first test in psychology, but there's a quiz on Monday on a whole new chapter, and I need to study for it. I brought along my textbook today to study in the quiet moments. My boss never minds as long as we keep an eye on things; It's one of the best things about working here.

My mind flashes back to Heather as I look around the room. I don't usually take people on private, free tours of the lighthouse, but there was something about her. She was so beautiful with her light-pink hair cascading down her back like a princess. She wore it in two space buns on the top of her head with the rest flowing with loose curls. I was shocked as hell when she wanted to take pictures of me. I'm certainly no model.

"Hi, Sage." Todd smiles as he walks in. He's the summer hire, fresh out of high school and about to go away to college.

"Hi Todd." I smile as he goes to clock in. He's six minutes late, but I'm not going to say anything. As long as he's here, we'll be fine. To be honest, this job is something I could do on my own, too, but I don't mind the company.

Todd comes out of the office, sliding his green tour shirt over his existing white T-shirt. He looks at the to-do list for the day and opens the front doors. No one is here yet or even waiting, but it's good to be open on time. He slips onto a chair and logs onto the cash register and then pulls out his phone. I put down the schedule, throw out my power bar wrapper, and finish off my iced coffee.

"I'm going to make sure the lighthouse is locked," I tell Todd and he nods, not looking up from his phone.

The lighthouse needs to stay locked from the public because it has a loose floorboard on the stairs that the boss refuses to fix. He said it's a liability having people up there anyway, so there's no reason to fix it anytime soon. I check that the rope is there, and then I slip past it, watching out for the loose floorboard—number six—and unlock the door to the top floor. Looking out at the water, I smile. Sometimes, when it isn't busy, I sneak up here just to have a moment to look at the water. It's one of the reasons I moved out of New York

City and came here. I need to be near the water. I need a break from the craziness, and I want to slow down a bit. Apparently that's only possible when I'm overlooking this water.

Sighing lightly, I lock the door and head back downstairs. I don't want Todd to go looking for me and find me up there. I slip under the rope and back to the main floor. No one is here except for Todd, who looks like he's playing a video game on his phone. I grab my textbook and hide out in the office, studying until a few minutes before our first tour group arrives. Then I go pee, chew a quick piece of gum, and wait for my tour in the designated area near the museum.

Heather pops into my head while I'm giving the tour. I can't help thinking about the extra facts I told her just to have something to say to her. I couldn't tell if she was just being nice or really wanted to hear about it at first, but considering she stuck it out with me, I'm impressed. I wonder if that pink-haired babe is going to show up again soon. Many locals like hanging out here, but maybe she's just a one-timer. All the more reason to add her on Instagram for the chance to see her again. I shake the thought from my head and answer the older woman's question about where the bathroom is for the third time. I repeat myself and say, "If you need to go, there's no need to announce it."

When the tour is over, I have a quick lunch, courtesy of my weekly meal prep. It's a perfect taco salad. I have about an hour of spare time tonight to hit the gym before showering and going out with Maeve and her friends. I like going to the gym a few times a week to stay in shape. Having abs and muscular biceps is something I train for. My meal prep helps me with time, but it also helps me to stay fit.

Todd takes the second tour, and I watch the register for a bit. No one comes, so I'm able to read the whole chapter a second time to really make sure it's sinking in. I'm looking for my phone in my pocket when I come across Heather's business card again. I'm not sure why I have it with me or why I'm overthinking it so much. It's simple really; I add her on Instagram, she sends me a few photos, and I say thanks and we move on. It's not like it's going to turn into something just because I think she's beautiful.

I think about texting Maeve to see what she thinks about the whole situation, but I already know what she'd say. She'd be convinced something was going on, and she'd tell me I should definitely reach out so I could get laid—her words, not mine. She's too worried about my sex life for her own good. I'm just not like that. Sure, I like sex but I like it better when I know I'll be seeing the person again. Hook-up culture has ruined sex for me. I don't want to hook-up with just anyone. That may work for Maeve and others, which is cool, but it just isn't for me. What if Heather just wants a hookup? Ugh, I don't even know this woman. I shouldn't be speculating about anything.

I decide to check out her Instagram before deciding whether or not to *follow* her. First green flag is the pride flag in her bio, so at least that answers one question. I scroll down to her photos, and the last one is a photo of the *Welcome to Lovers* sign at the beginning of town. She doesn't caption her posts; she just uses hashtags. I swipe through unfamiliar faces of people who could be models or just friends of hers. There's really no way to know. She takes photos of architecture and water too, not just people, but they're all edited in a subtle way that makes it her style. The photos are nice, but I'm careful not to accidentally like any of them. Been there, made that mistake before.

"Excuse me? Can I buy a ticket?" an older gentleman asks, startling me out of my thoughts. I drop my phone on the counter and switch back into work-mode.

"Of course! That'll be five-fifty." I smile and ring him up. He hands me some cash, and I slip it into the drawer exchanging it for a ticket.

"Thank you." He nods and slowly starts walking toward the museum.

I reach for my phone, click *follow* on her profile, and then set my phone down. Of course, anytime my phone buzzes for the next several hours, I'm jumping to check it. It's incredibly unlike me, but I'm curious to see if she'll *follow* me back. Eventually, work ends.

Todd leaves a little early, and I lock up behind him. I drive over to the gym, change into some sweats, and turn my anxiety into exercise. I might be overdoing it, because anytime Heather pops into my head, I do another twenty crunches. Sure, I might not have a pretty girl following me back, but I'll be ripped.

"Hey, I was wondering if you could spot me?" a blonde I've seen here before asks. She's a few inches shorter and smiles with her teeth. A deep blush creeps over her cheeks from lifting the weights onto the bar.

"Sure." I nod. I'm done with my workout for the day anyway.

I follow behind her, and she takes a deep breath before lifting the bar. She does several squats before placing it on the ground. She doesn't even seem out of breath, and only a few blonde hairs are out of place from her pony tail.

"I'm Julie, by the way."

"Oh, right. I'm Sage." I smile and extend a hand. I can't help but notice how sweaty hers is.

"Do you mind if I go again?"

"Nah, go for it." I nod. This time, I notice the guys around her all staring. She is kind of cute, wearing tight spandex and lifting more than she weighs. It's impressive.

"That was good," I say when she's done.

"Thank you, I've been training for a while."

"It's obvious by your form."

"Can I be honest for a second?" She chews on her bottom lip.

"Sure, what's up?"

"I didn't ask you to spot me because I needed one. I could've asked anyone, but I think you're cute so I was hoping to break the ice. Maybe we can get a drink or something?"

"I'd—" I'm about to agree when my phone buzzes. I glance at it quickly.

Heather has followed you back

"Something important?" she asks, raising an eyebrow.

"Yeah, thank you. But I don't think I can. Maybe another time." I leave before she has a chance to respond. I grab my gym bag and head to my car. Clicking on the notification, I feel my heart swelling.

I don't know what comes over me, it's probably the endorphins from my workout, but I quickly type a short message and press *send* before I can overthink it. Just like Julie, I'm putting myself out there and shooting my shot. Hopefully it'll go a little bit better than it went for her. I smile, at least knowing I tried—and that's one of the hardest things about getting back out there.

FIVE

Heather

I had been waiting a few days when Sage's following notification popped up on my phone. Of course I wasn't near my phone when it first popped up, so I didn't have to play it cool and wait to *follow* her back. I took a peek at her page, which is mainly photos of the Lovers Lighthouse and a few with some friends, but that's it. She doesn't have too many posts, and her page is set to private, so I had to wait for her to accept my follow request to even look.

I make a mental note to send the photos of her when I get home from coffee with the girls today. They're sitting on my computer, edited and ready to be sent over. I already let Sage know they would be coming today, so I'm sure she'll be waiting for them. What I didn't expect was her to ask me out so quickly. Well, I don't know if it was a date exactly. The wording of it was super unclear and now that I think about it, she might just be trying to be nice. She does have a pride flag in her bio, so it's at least promising that she's probably more than an ally. I click on her profile and re-read the message she sent me.

SAGE:

Would you be interested in a private tour of the lighthouse before it opens? You could probably get some great shots of the sunrise if you come early enough.

ME:

That sounds amazing! Just tell me when 😊

SAGE:

How does tomorrow morning sound? Let's meet in the parking lot around 4:45 a.m.

ME:

Perfect!

Nowhere in it does she say it's a date or anything more than her helping me out, considering she has special privileges. So I try not to get my hopes up. Closing my phone, I change into a strapless light-green romper and a pair of white Converse. I check the time and realize I need to head out. Love in a Cup, the cafe is just in town but it's often a pain in the ass to find a parking spot. I grab my keys and my camera and hop in my car.

Five minutes later, I'm pulling into the parking lot and regretting not leaving sooner. It's dumb to have one parking lot so close to three small businesses and another parking lot that's almost a ten minute walk away from everything. I know I could walk, but it's hot as hell today, and the last thing I want is to show up to seeing my friends all sweaty. After driving in circles around the parking lot, someone is finally pulling out of a spot, so I grab it at the last second. Checking my hair in the mirror, I fix a loose strand and then head into the coffee shop.

Looking around the small shop, I realize my friends aren't here yet, so I walk up to the counter and order an iced matcha tea. I'm not the biggest fan of coffee; something about the taste is just too strong, and it gives me a killer headache.

"HEATHER!" My name is called so loudly, everyone turns around and looks at the door. One of my best and oldest friends, Ryleigh, is standing in the doorway with a wide, outstretched smile on her face.

"Ry Ry!" I leave my tea behind and run into my best friends arms. She's the tiniest of all of us, barely five feet, so her head leans into my chest as we hug. Her long, dark curls are piled half up in a bun on top of her head, the rest flowing freely down her back. She's wearing a cute floral spring dress and a pair of ballet flats.

"How are you?" She smiles and lets go of me.

"I'm so good. It's been too long," I say.

"Am I just chopped liver then?" Alana asks, lowering her dark shades.

"Oh, stop it." I roll my eyes and hug my best friend. I just saw her a few days ago, and we'd had as big of a reunion as Ryleigh and I had.

"Go grab your tea before someone steals it," Alana teases. They get in line to grab their drinks, and I look for a table that will accommodate the four of us. Kim is the only one of the group who isn't in town yet. She's coming sometime next month. She can't get out of her apartment lease any sooner.

I find a table toward the back and sit in the booth side of the table. Sipping my drink, I smile, pleased with the drink. It's often hit or miss with tea, especially at most coffee shops—who obviously specialize in coffee.

"Is Norah coming?" I ask as Ryleigh and Alana take a seat across from me.

"Yeah, she said she would be a few minutes late."

"Did you both find dates to the wedding yet?" Alana glances at her phone just as I see Norah walk in. She waves shyly and steps in line to order a coffee.

"How's she doing?" I ask quietly. The last time I saw her, and the last time we were all together, was at her husband's funeral early last year. It was sudden and unexpected, and we all rallied behind Norah, taking turns staying with her until we ran out of time-off.

"She's better, but she doesn't want to talk about him," Alana says softly.

"Understandable." I nod. I couldn't imagine going through life after losing the love of your life.

"Norah!" I jump up and greet my redheaded best friend with a hug. She has a softness about her that's always been there, but she also has a quality that I can't quite describe. The best way to explain it? I want to hug her and not let go.

"Hey gals." She smiles and sits down with her drink. It doesn't look like coffee; maybe some kind of a tea?

"How are things going with the wedding?" Norah steers the conversation away her and to Alana. I don't blame her; I'm sure it's been hard with everyone looking at her since her loss.

"They, uh, could be better." Alana sighs. "It's like Will and I never have any time alone since all of our friends and family are in town. I won't be sad when it's all over."

"Are you getting along with his family?" Ryleigh asks.

"Yes and no. They're just trying to have a lot of say, and it's been causing a bit of tension between Will and I. I've joked about just running to town hall and eloping to forget about the whole business."

"Really?" I ask, surprised. As long as we've known Alana all she's talked about is the big wedding and ceremony she wants to have. I can't imagine her in town hall with just one or two of us there.

"Well, no. But something has to give. It just doesn't feel like us anymore. I'm sure it's just the pre-wedding jitters or something." She shrugs, shaking it off as she takes a hearty sip of her coffee.

"Is it weird being back in town?" Norah asks me.

"Not really. I just hope I can find an apartment in town sooner than later," I admit. I love living at Alana's parents' guest house, but I want my own space.

"Yeah, that's why I've been staying at the other house on the property—it's been tough trying to find a space in town. Besides, I don't know if I just want an apartment or a house or what. I'm kind of in this limbo of moving on," Norah admits. She moved back several months ago, getting a job at the local book store until she's back on her feet.

"Well, you both are welcome to stay as long as you want," Alana promises.

"Got another house for me?" Ryleigh jokes.

"I mean, you could stay with Wrenn. She's staying in one for the summer, and the last house is in the process of being renovated. It got flooded earlier this year," Alana explains.

Ryleigh makes a face at the mention of Alana's little sister. Does she know something we don't? I know she's always been annoyed by Alana's little sister, but surely she's outgrown that by now, right?

"Oh shit, what time is our appointment?" Ryleigh changes the conversation casually. I make a mental note to ask her about Wrenn later.

"Crap, we gotta get going," Alana laughs, checking her Apple Watch. We're all supposed to try on bridesmaid dresses for the wedding.

"You said it's in the town over, right? Are we all driving or just taking one car?" I ask.

"I have to head home right after, but you're all welcome to drive together," Alana says, still texting.

"I can drive if you're both okay with it. I'm parked right out front," I suggest.

"Sounds good to me," Ryleigh and Norah agree.

Twenty minutes later, we're pulling into the parking lot of *Mama's Dresses and Designs*. It's a bigger boutique than I expected, but it's cute. The second we get inside, Alana is already there talking to someone, so we huddle by the front, waiting for her.

"Would you like any champagne?" A woman walks over to us with a smile.

"No, thanks," I say politely. I have to drive home, and I haven't eaten much today.

"I'll have one," Ryleigh says as Norah declines hers. It's not surprising; I can't remember the last time I saw her with a drink in her hand.

"Okay, so they're pulling the dresses I picked for you guys. I have an idea of what I think you'd choose, but it's totally up to you. Any of these five dresses can be turned into the colors of the wedding, which are navy blue and gray," Alana says, smiling and picking up a glass of champagne.

"Do we get to see your dress?" Norah asks curiously.

"I hadn't even thought about that, but let me ask if they can pull that for us too," Alana says excitedly. I'm surprised she hadn't had it prepared to show us. She loves showing off, and a wedding dress means all the focus should be on her. She disappears to track down the woman, and we look around the shop. Another family is looking at wedding dresses together across the shop.

"Okay, so she had me pull these, and we have them in a multitude of sizes. We can have you tell us however you're comfortable," the woman says, gesturing to a rack full of colorful dresses, each in different styles.

Ryleigh, Norah, and I look at each one slowly, wanting to take it all in before requesting sizes in any of the dresses. They all have a similar look—spaghetti straps, a silky feeling, and a long length.

"Can I see this one in a size six?" Ryleigh asks. The woman nods, then looks at Norah and me.

"Can I see these two in a size four?" Norah pulls out two different dresses.

"And you?" The woman looks at me, and I pause.

"Can I see the last one and the first one?" Then I step closer and whisper my size to the woman. I'm not ashamed of my number; I fought like hell to get to a place where I felt that. But I also don't want to worry about my friends silently comparing. Not that they're the type to do that, but this is the hazard of being in eating disorder recovery. I try to avoid anything that might trigger me into an episode.

The woman disappears just as Alana walks out with another woman who's holding the train of her dress. Norah audibly gasps while Ryleigh and I look on in awe. Alana looks beautiful; it's long-sleeved but dips down to show off her ample cleavage. The dress is white but has an upper layer of lace flowers covering her arms and chest. It flows all around her like a princess gown.

"Wow. You look amazing," Norah is the first to speak, with Ryleigh and I adding our praises.

"Thank you, it took forever to find it. And they still have to hem a few spots, but I think this is the one," Alana says anxiously, looking down. It's one of the first times I've ever seen her look nervous. But it's normal to be nervous about getting married, right?

SIX

Sage

I don't know why I'm freaking out so much, but my palms are sweaty and I've almost dropped the keys to the lighthouse about three times now. It's 4:43 a.m., and I've been here for thirteen minutes, arriving incredibly early because I couldn't help myself. I don't want Heather to be waiting around for me or anything. My leg is shaking as I sit on the bench outside the lighthouse. I probably shouldn't have chugged that iced coffee on the way here, but I didn't sleep very well. I was up half the night staring at the photos Heather took. She sent over the photos she took of me, and there were a ton of them. I went through each of them, one by one, paying attention to the details she captured. She managed to make me look hot? Is that okay to say? Well, who cares. I *am* fucking hot.

I went on a deep dive, checking out her website and any other social media she has. It's pretty clear—from the semi-stalking I did—that she isn't currently seeing anyone, but it is possible that she was involved with someone not too long ago. Not that this is a date or anything. I don't want to risk not being able to see her again, so I used neutral language about today. I want to get to know her better before I ask her out on a date. I know it's a little old-fashioned, but five minutes of conversation and cyberstalking isn't enough to know if I like someone.

"Hey! I'm here!" Heather calls from across the parking lot. She's waving her hand in the air wildly and carrying a black bag with the other.

"Hey!" I call back. I stand up and let go of a breath.

"Thank you so much for this, I'm so excited." She has her pink hair in a messy bun on the top of her head, and she's wearing minimal makeup, which just shows her natural beauty. Her bright-blue eyes pop even brighter than the other day, and I notice some light freckles across her cheeks.

"Of course." I smile. The lighthouse doesn't open for several hours, and I know we'll be out of here way before then. The security cameras aren't hooked up, and I know the code for the alarm system, so there's no way we'll get caught. And for once, I'm not so worried about following the rules.

I lead Heather inside and around the side before stopping. "Do you want to see the sunrise from somewhere different?" I ask.

"Sure, I'm up for whatever." She smiles.

"Okay, follow me." I unlock the lighthouse doors, turn off the alarm system, and lead her up to the third floor where everything is off-limits. "Watch your step there." I point out the faulty step.

"Thanks." She carefully steps over it and follows me as I unlock the last doors.

"Wow," she whispers quietly. I flip on the light switch, but I didn't expect it to turn on; it hasn't been used in years.

"There are no lights, but the windows open," I explain and unhook the window to show the view in front of us. The sun isn't ready to come up yet, but the waves are crashing against the shore, and the breeze comes in lightly. I glance at Heather, and despite her short-shorts, she's prepared on top with a jean jacket over her outfit.

"It's amazing, I've never been up here before."

"It's off-limits because of the step, but as long as you don't fall or anything, we should be fine," I joke.

"Got it, thankfully I'm not too clumsy." She laughs.

"Do you need any help setting anything up?" I ask, looking at the bag she's holding.

"No thanks, just sit back and relax." She starts taking out lenses and laying them in front of her on the windowsill. She sets up her camera on the settings she wants, and it's then I notice the peek of the sun starting to rise from behind the water.

"This was perfect timing." Heather smiles.

"Sometimes I come up here before work and watch the sunrise. It's relaxing," I admit.

"This is my favorite place in town. If I had access to up here, I'd never leave."

"What is it for you?" I ask curiously.

"The waves. There's something about them always manages to calm me down. It's like all my stress just goes out to sea with each new wave. What about you?"

I smile. "That's what it is for me, too. I can clear my thoughts up here. I put a lot of pressure on myself, and it's like all of that is gone when I'm here."

"Exactly. It's something I missed greatly when I moved away. I'm happy to be back," Heather says in between shots. I'm trying to watch the sunrise, but my eyes are glued to her. She looks so beautiful in her element. Relaxed and calm, she's taking everything in from a unique perspective, and I can't wait to see how these photos come out.

"Where did you live before here?"

"Well, I'm born and raised in Lovers. But I moved to Vermont for college. I have a scholarship and wanted to venture out on my own for a bit. How about you?"

"I'm originally from New York. I moved here a few years ago… for a change." I don't mention my mom; it would be too much too soon. I mean, you don't trauma dump on the first date, even if this isn't officially a date.

"Are you a tour guide full time?" she asks.

"No, I mean I work here a lot, borderline on full-time, but no. I'm a grad student at the University of Maine."

"Nice, what for?"

"I'm going for social work."

"Wow, tough major. I took a few psych classes in college, but it was too rough for me to continue. Do you want to be a social worker, or are you aiming for something else in the field?"

"Social worker. I'm not sure exactly what aspect I want to work in, but I have a few months to decide." I'm supposed to graduate in the fall, so at some point before then, I have to choose which direction my career is going in.

"Gotcha, I respect the hell out of you for that. It's a lot tougher than, say, pointing a camera at the ocean and editing them," she adds with a laugh.

"It's surely different. But I could never do what you do; I don't have a creative bone in my body. Besides, that mural you captured? That's breathtaking."

Heather stops taking photos, looks at me quizzically, and then smirks.

"What?"

"Sage, did you stalk me?" She raises an eyebrow at me with a smile.

"W-what?" I stumble over my words. How does she know that?

"The photos of the mural aren't on my Instagram. They're on my website. A few months back, by the way." She laughs and I'm sure my cheeks are the color of her hair. If I could sink into the floor, I would.

"I-uh." I rub the back of my bare neck and wince.

"It's okay, I cyberstalked you too." She winks and I let out a sigh of relief from being let off the hook.

"Oh," I say. It's all I can manage. What do you say when a beautiful girl admits to cyberstalking you?

"I was meeting you in the dark by a lighthouse; I just needed to make sure you weren't some kind of murderer," she teases.

"Shit, I didn't even think about how that might come across. I'm shocked you agreed."

"Eh, I figured, what's the chance you'd actually kill me?" She laughs.

"For the record, I'm not a murderer. Blood makes me queasy or I'd have gone into nursing," I admit.

"Well that's good."

It's quiet for a bit while we both look at the sunrise. She's snapping away, and I just watch the water and the pink and purple sky behind it.

"So you're in town for a wedding, right?" I ask, hoping I remembered correctly.

"Yup, my best friend Alana is getting married." She smiles.

"Are you in the wedding party?"

"Yes! I'm a bridesmaid with a few of our best friends. We actually just got fitted for our dresses yesterday."

"Oh nice, do you like them or are they like totally ugly?"

"No, Alana loves us so she let us pick which style would look best on us. She just choose the color."

"That's good. I was once in a wedding party where I had to wear the most ridiculous dress. Which is an issue in the first place because I hate wearing dresses. It's safe to say I don't talk to that friend anymore."

"Oh man, I'm so sorry. Alana said she wants us to be happy in what we wear. My friend, Norah, did a similar thing when she got married, there were a few choices for us. I truly think it's the best way to go, I mean, everyone is so different and has different body types."

"That's such a good point. Are you excited for the wedding?"

"Umm…" Heather sighs.

"What?" I ask, then add, "If I'm prying we can totally change the subject."

"No, it's so stupid. I'm excited for the wedding. But my ex is in the groom's wedding party so I have to see her, and I'm not looking forward to that at all." She frowns.

"Damn, I'm guessing a bad breakup?"

"Yeah, she cheated on me a few months back. Oh my gosh, I'm so sorry. I don't know why I'm telling you all this." She shakes her head. "It's not your problem or your worry. I'm just stressed about running into them and finding a date for the wedding."

"Ah." I can understand that. Running into your ex is not fun, especially when they might be with someone new. When I run into Macey with one of the guys she cheated on me with, it feels like a gut punch. But at least I can leave the cafeteria and not have to converse with her. I can't imagine going to a wedding and needing to play nice with them in front of all my friends.

"Yeah, so if you know anyone who wants to pull up to a wedding with me. Shit I'd even settle for someone who'd just show up my ex at this point," she says with a laugh.

But a light clicks in my head. I could do that. Showing up to the wedding with Heather on my arm just for her to show her ex she's moved on? Why would I pass up that opportunity? It would give me the chance to get to know Heather better without the pressure of actually dating. And who knows, maybe as we get to know each other things would happen on their own. I mean, you never know, right?

"I'm down," I say aloud.

"Wait. What?" Heather's head snaps around to stare at me with her jaw dropped.

"You need a date, and I'm available," I say with a shrug. *Be casual*, I coach myself.

"You're serious?" she asks, surprised.

"Yeah, why not? Your friends don't know me, so it would be believable. I'm not doing much this summer, and I'd love to get to know you more. I'm happy to help you make a shitty ex jealous and prove you're over them."

"Damn, I wasn't being serious. But I also can't think of a single reason why this wouldn't be a good idea." She pauses. "I just don't know if showing up to the wedding with you would be enough, though."

"What do you mean?"

"I just don't know if they'd believe it if we're never seen together before the wedding. I wouldn't want it to be suspicious if I've never mentioned you or introduced you to anyone before." She chews on her bottom lip.

I think about it for a moment. Maeve's voice pops into my head, telling me to go for it. She said I need to get out more, to have more of a social life. I know what I'm about to say is crazy, but hell, maybe that's what I need. There's something about Heather that makes me want to jump head first into whatever with her.

"So, I'll be your fake girlfriend, then. We can spend the summer making our relationship public and believable before showing up at the wedding."

"You'd do that?"

"Why not?"

Heather hesitates. I can see her mind working overtime while thinking about it. I don't blame her, this isn't something you should just jump into impulsively—like I'm doing.

"What's your last name?" she asks suddenly.

"What?" I look at her, confused.

"If you're going to be my fake girlfriend, I think I should at least know your last name," she says with a glimmer in her eye. Holy shit, we're really going to do this.

"Brooks." I smile as she nods. It's like signing an invisible contract. I glance out the window at the fully round sun, wondering how I just got myself into this.

SEVEN

Heather

"Okay, so the bride wants me to tell you she needs a few shots of her family before she walks down the aisle," the wedding planner tells me. I've forgotten her name, but I think it starts with a J…maybe Jane? Janet?

"Sure." I nod. Did I really need to know her name?

I pick up my camera, dust off my knees from kneeling in the grass, and look around for the bride's family. I was introduced to everyone last night at the rehearsal dinner, but I'm not the best with names—clearly. The bride is a short brunette, so I look for anyone similar that I recognize. Ah, there they are at the end of the aisle fixing the dad's tie.

"Hi! Trina asked if I could get some shots of you guys before the wedding?" I smile as I walk up to the family.

"Of course!" Her mom jumps into position, standing in front of the view of the ocean. Her youngest daughter and son stand by her sides while her husband stands on the end.

I grab a few shots, thank them, and head back inside to find the bride. It's almost time for her to be walked down the aisle, and I don't want to miss anything. They don't want any "getting ready" pictures, which makes my day a hell of a lot easier. I don't have to worry about setting up flat lays or worrying about missing the first moments of the ceremony.

"Did you get the family shots?" Trina asks, walking over to me. The room is utter chaos; her bridesmaids are running around the room and clearly looking for something.

"Yes, I'm all ready for when you come down the aisle." I nod.

"Perfect!" She looks back. "Guys, it's fine. I'll just go down the aisle in no panties, it's not like anyone will know." Trina waves off her friends and picks up a mimosa.

I leave them to figure out the panties situation and head back outside. I grab a spot at the back of the aisle so I'll be able to get the angles she wants. Fifteen hot minutes later, the groom and the wedding parties make their way outside. I wish I wasn't dressed so warmly, but it's standard that I wore an all-black outfit to blend into the background. Trina makes her way down the aisle, and then I follow suit, grabbing the shots of the back of her dress and her dad holding onto her.

The wedding ceremony starts, but I mainly tune it out. I need to focus on getting these shots right. Not to mention, I'm crouching at all kinds of angles to make sure I'm not obstructing anyone's view. At least it's not as long as some of the ceremonies I've been to. Sometimes they drone on for hours, and by the end, people are bored out of their minds.

Shooting at weddings isn't my favorite thing to do, but it definitely pays the bills. Doing one to three weddings a month allows me to keep the lifestyle I want and has paid off majority of my student debt. I do more weddings in the summer to keep up with the slower months, so I'm used to the ordeal here. Plus, I'm pretty good at doing my job and staying focused. They kiss and I almost miss it because at the last second, some old guy almost blocks my shot, but thankfully, I jump up and get it. Don't people know not to block the photographer?

My phone buzzes a few times in my pocket, but I ignore it. It's on for emergencies, but I'm not going to miss a shot to answer a random text. Wait, is it Sage? I gave her my number yesterday after we agreed to our silly little plan. I mean, I still think it's a crazy idea that we won't pull off. But on the other hand, Sage had made some good points. Besides, I'm a little selfish. I only said yes so I could keep hanging out with Sage. She's hot and funny, and there's something about her that just makes her super easy to talk to. I'm not saying I'm fully crushing on her, but damn...I'm incredibly attracted to her, to say the least. And spending more time with her would not be a chore in the slightest.

I'm thinking about checking my phone when Trina pulls me from my thoughts. She waves me over to where she's smiling with her new husband, Wyatt. The way he's staring at her when she's not even looking is telling of how much he loves her. I've shot a ton of weddings, and I've also done some shoots for women and men getting divorced. Separately, of course. But I can usually tell on the wedding day if this is a couple I'll have to shoot again.

"I know we didn't talk about this, but could we get some extra shots of just Wyatt and I with the water behind us? We didn't know the sun would be setting at this time." Trina forces a smile.

"Of course." I nod. I wasn't about to deny a bride what she wanted. Besides, a few extra photos wasn't going to kill anyone.

I tell them to be natural and Wyatt looks nervous, but suddenly Trina whispers something in his ear, and he blushes then kisses her passionately. It's an amazing photo, and I wonder what Trina told him. I have a pretty good idea, though. After the sun officially sets, we join the reception inside, and I grab a plate of food. I usually survive on granola bars on these things, but Trina was kind enough to make sure I got some food in me. After gorging on the veggies and bread, the only vegan options, I make a mental note to grab something on the way home. I know I won't feel like cooking by the time I got home. I chug a bottle of water and get back to work.

I'm heading to my car when I'm stopped by one of the men coming from the wedding. He smiles as he flags me down.

"Hey, I was hoping to catch you," he says as he catches up. He's universally attractive with his dark hair and chiseled jawline. I'm not attracted to men, and even I think he's hot. Is he coming to hit on me? I hope not. It's always awkward letting guys down gently.

"What's up?" I smile as I face him.

"I'm looking to propose to my girlfriend; she's here so I couldn't stop you inside. I'd love to grab your card or something if you have one. I want someone to capture the engagement," he explains.

"Oh, yeah, of course." I click open the trunk, put my camera and supplies away, and grab a card for him. After I hand it to him, he reads it and smiles.

"Heather. Nice. I'll definitely be contacting you! I'm Ethan, by the way."

"Sounds good." He takes off toward the party, and I finish packing up for the day.

I map the way home on my phone, adding in a quick stop at Teddy's. I place an order on the phone while I'm driving and hope it'll be ready by the time I get there. I can't wait to get home, change into some sweats, and lounge on the couch for the night. There is a reality show waiting to be binged calling my name. I pull into the parking lot of the bar, taking in how busy it is, and I mentally remember it's a Saturday night. I should've gone through the McDonald's drive-through or something. It's too late now, so I sigh, wishing I had at least brought a change of clothes.

Teddy's is crowded, even for a Saturday night. The booths are filled with people drinking and eating, meanwhile, the bar is crowded with people looking for drinks. The hostess stand is empty, so I head farther inside to find someone to help me. There's music playing over the speakers, and although there isn't an official dance floor, everyone seems to have made one in the middle of Teddy's. I make my way to the end of the bar and wait my turn to ask about my food. Wrenn spots me and holds up a finger, letting me know she sees me, and I nod.

"What can I get ya?" She walks over and smiles at me.

"I'm just picking up an order of food."

"Gotcha! I'll run to the kitchen and grab it."

"Thanks!" I call after her.

I step out of the way so the people behind me can order their drinks from the other bartenders. My phone is in the car, so I just glance around the room while I wait. Thankfully, there's no one I recognize and I don't think anyone recognizes me. I hate having to make small talk with someone I went to high school with over a decade ago. My eyes find the couple dancing in the middle of the room, there's something familiar about them. Their partner pushes their dark hair behind their ear, and I freeze.

Quickly, I look away, hoping I haven't been spotted. I was so stupid to think I could go somewhere in town and not run into someone. I was stupid to think I wouldn't run into *her*. I haven't seen Jane in months, not since our inevitable breakup when I found her tongue deep in another woman's pussy. I slammed the door on her and ignored her pleas at attempting to explain. Clearly, things aren't any different. I can't be sure, seeing as this woman is clothed, but I am fairly certain this is the woman she cheated on me with. I know they made it official a few weeks after we broke up, but that's all I know. Besides knowing she'd be at Alana's wedding, that was the extent of my knowledge. I want it that way. The less I know, the better.

"Here you are!, I packed some extra sauce for the wait," Wrenn says, holding the bag of food in front of me.

"Thanks, see you soon." I smile. Glancing up one last time, I lock eyes with the woman who was dancing with Jane. I don't know if she recognizes me or not because she just blinks and looks away.

I all but run out of the bar. The last thing I want is an encounter with Jane right now. After making it to my car, I drive all the way home and don't breathe until I'm inside. I know she didn't follow me or anything, but damn, that whole encounter put me on edge. It's never ideal to run into your ex, but I at least want to look good when it happens.

Sage pops into my head. Hot and sweet Sage. I want her to be there the first time I run into Jane. I'll be all made up in my brides-maid dress, and Sage will be wearing a suit. I'll feel confident on her arm, and running into Jane won't matter because I'll have moved on

—at least to the outside world. I decide to send her a quick text. If this is going to work, we need to plan this right. We should get to know each other better, and that calls for spending some time together.

ME:

Are you free this week? I think we should get to know each other better so there's no mishaps

SAGE:

Sounds good, how's tomorrow work?

ME:

I have photos to edit...

SAGE:

I have a paper to work on, can we make it a working day?

ME:

I love the sound of that. Why don't you come over around 11?

I send her my address, and she replies with a thumbs up. I feel a little better knowing the two of us will be on the same page. I mean, that's how a fake relationship is supposed to work, *right?*

EIGHT

Sage

"So you're going to her house?!" Maeve squeals with joy from the other end of my phone. She was on speaker, but it isn't like anyone is around to hear.

"Yes, and I'm incredibly nervous."

"I can imagine! Did you shave?"

"I—Excuse me?!" My voice gets caught in my throat.

"What? I mean you don't have to, it's 2024, but at least make it accessible. It's been so long since you've had sex; I didn't know if it's jungle-like down there."

"Maeve!" I squeal, begging her to stop. My face is bright-red in mortification. I cannot be having this conversation right now.

"What? Isn't that why you called?"

"No!" I yell. "I was nervous about going over, but not because of that. We're not having sex."

"Oh, then why are you nervous?"

I hadn't yet explained the whole "fake dating" thing to Maeve. I'm not sure if I'm allowed, and if I am, how do I even explain it? I kinda like this girl, but I'm too chicken to ask her out, so instead I'm pretending to date her in hopes that we fall in love?

"Sage?" Maeve prompts.

"I'm just nervous to be alone with her. It's not like either of us have called it a date, but I don't know that it's *not* a date…if that makes sense."

"It does, maybe she's feeling the same way. And that's okay. Just be yourself and go with the flow. What are you two doing at her house if not making use of her bed?"

"She said she has photos to edit, and I have that paper to work on so we're just being casual. We're getting to know each other," I add, thinking about her text from last night. It's a good idea for us to get to know each other so there's no room for error at the wedding.

"Okay, so just be yourself and get to know her. If you're nervous then just keep asking her questions and keep her talking."

"That's a good idea."

"I have those from time to time." She laughs.

"Thank you. I should get going. I don't want to be late," I say, looking at the clock on my nightstand.

"Okay. Bye! Have fun!" She clicks goodbye, and I grab my phone off the charger.

Picking up my backpack, I throw a few last minute items inside and head to Heather's apartment. I know this isn't her house, but damn…I'm impressed. It's huge and beautiful. I've been to the estates before, but just once. It was when I got lost shortly after moving here. Still, it was nothing compared to seeing them up close. They're kind of intimidating.

"Hey, you made it." Heather walks out in a pair of white shorts that show off her long legs and a loose tank top. The wind blows, and it becomes obvious that she's not wearing a bra. I know I shouldn't be looking, but it's not like I'm being a creep. I distract my thoughts and lock the car behind me.

"It's beautiful here," I say, clearing my throat.

"I love it! Alana's letting me stay for the summer. It's just until I find my own apartment in Lovers. It's proving harder than I expected it to be." She shrugs.

I nod and walk inside—which is just as beautiful. Looking around, I see Heather's claimed a spot on the couch with a laptop and a pile of photos on the table.

"Come in and make yourself comfortable. I'm going to get us some snacks. Any allergies?" She asks closing the front door. I notice that her bright hair is down in loose curls; she looks relaxed here.

"Nope, well technically, I shouldn't have too much dairy. But I'm not worried about it," I admit.

"Gotcha." She smiles. I'm one of those lactose intolerant people who should avoid dairy, but I play with the limit of how much I have. I'm fine most of the time.

I take a seat on the white couch across from where she's set up and start to pull out my laptop and textbook. Heather comes back with a small charcuterie board of snacks and places it on the coffee table between us.

"I know it's probably too much, but I didn't know what you like. And I like to snack while I work."

"It's great, thanks." I take a bagel chip and a piece of cheddar cheese.

"Oh, drinks! Do you want water or lemonade?"

"Lemonade sounds great." I smile. I couldn't remember the last time someone offered me lemonade.

Heather nods and retreats into the kitchen again. I look around the room; it's very light and open. The windows are oversized and provide an abundance of natural light. There's no photos around, nothing that makes this place look more than an Airbnb. But it makes sense. If she's just here for the summer, she isn't going to take the time to redecorate someone else's space.

"Here you are." Heather hands me a glass with lemonade, and I take a small sip. She hands me a wooden coaster, and I place it on the table lightly.

Heather sits cross-legged on the other couch and pulls her laptop on her lap. I expected to have some sort of conversation, but I guess we're just jumping into work? Maybe she didn't have much to say to me? It's a little odd, but just as I'm about to open my textbook, she speaks.

"So what's your paper on?"

"It's for psychology, so I'm writing about the effects of foster care long-term."

"Oh, I can't imagine that's a happy paper." She frowns.

"Not really, but it's the reality of it."

She nods.

"Are these wedding photos?" I ask, glancing at the pile in front of her.

"Yup, I had a wedding last night actually. But these are from two weeks ago, I have to get them some proofs to look at before I send the final copies," she explains.

"Gotcha, how was the wedding last night?"

"*So* good! I even got offered a job shooting an engagement last night."

"Wow, that's awesome right?"

"Yeah, it definitely pays the bills. They're not my favorite things to shoot, but I like them a lot."

"What is your favorite thing to shoot?" I ask curiously.

"Landscapes, like when we did the sunrise shoot the other day. I'll have to show you those photos later; they came out amazing," she says proudly.

"I can't wait to see." I smile.

"I'm glad you could come over today," she says suddenly.

"I'm glad you asked."

"I'll be honest, I sort of ran into my ex last night..." She nervously looks away from me.

"Oh?"

"Yeah, I mean I saw her and her new girlfriend. I don't think she saw me, but the new girlfriend did and I don't know if she recognized me." Heather frowns.

"Are you okay?"

"I thought I was more over her than I was. But apparently it still hurts just as bad seeing it in person. Like they were just dancing together, and I felt like I'd been punched in the gut."

"I'm sorry." I know exactly what that feels like. I wouldn't wish that on anyone.

"It's alright. I just guess I'm not ready to date yet. I mean, I'm ready for *this*. But not anything more. It's too soon, I guess."

I take in what she's saying. It's a disappointment, but I'm not in any kind of rush. If she needs time to get over her ex and move on from things, I can wait.

"I've been cheated on, and sometimes it just takes a little time. But I'm sure when you're ready to try again, someone will be there who understands." I smile softly. She looks up, staring deep into my eyes, and I can't help but blush. There is something so intimate about the look we're sharing.

I'm the first to break the eye contact, and she clears her throat, taking a long sip of lemonade. "Well, we should get some work done."

"Sure." I nod and lean back on the couch, pulling the textbook back to my lap.

There are a few chapters I need to read before I can write my paper. I try to focus on what I'm reading, but it's hard when Heather is just a few feet away. I catch myself staring at her more than once, and I hope she doesn't catch on. She's just so beautiful; it's hard not to look at her. She's deep in editing mode, though, which I've learned incudes her reaching for snacks every thirty seconds and pulling her hair into a tight ponytail. It gives me a better look at her face, which is even more distracting, but I force myself to re-read the paragraph I'm on.

"Do you have a favorite snack?" she randomly asks.

"Uh, I like protein bars, but I guess they're not really a snack. I like apples and strawberries, too."

She stares at me like I have three heads.

"What?" I ask, confused.

"I mean like chips or cookies or something, not fruit." She frowns.

"Oh, I guess potato chips. I don't eat a lot of junk food." I shrug.

"I hate when people call it junk food." She sighs.

"What do you mean?"

"I—uh, had…well I guess *have* an eating disorder. I'm anorexic, and one of the things that bugs me the most is how people—not just you—distinguish food as good versus bad. It's just food. If you eat too many apples, you'll get a belly ache just as much as if you eat too many chips," Heather explains.

"That's a good point," I admit. I've never thought of it that way.

"I'm not saying to live off chips and cookies, but balance is important. That's all." She shrugs.

"Do you currently struggle with it?" I ask, hoping I'm not overstepping.

"No. I mean, yeah it's always there. But I've been in recovery for ten years, and I haven't had an issue for a long time. It's not something I like discussing often, but I also thought maybe you should know…considering our situation."

"Understandable." I make a mental note to Google some things later. I know enough about eating disorders, but I don't want to accidentally trigger her out of recovery. I'll feel better once I do some research about what might be common and what might help.

"If you have questions you can ask me."

"I—uh well, I don't want to assume anything. I'm just curious about a few things…" I admit.

"Go for it. It's a safe space, and I'm sure it's nothing I haven't been asked before." She smiles encouragingly.

"Do you have any trigger foods? Things to avoid, things I should avoid? Things I should know?"

"I don't like to avoid anything, but I try not to keep candy around since that was one of my trigger foods in the past. I'm a vegan, so that's just good information to know. I changed my diet to vegan in my process of recovery. It was a way for me to have control with food, but in a healthy way. I would just ask that you don't make a big deal of it. It's my issue, not for you to do or not do anything differently. Be yourself around me and we'll be good," she explains.

"Okay. I can do that." I smile. "But please don't make me eat any tofu. I had it once by accident, and it tasted like feet."

"Then the person who made it didn't know how to spice it correctly." Heather laughs. "But okay, no tofu for you." She relaxes.

"Do you want to see the photos I took at the lighthouse?"

"Sure." She effectively changes the subject, and I walk over to her couch.

She fluffs her hair back, and I get a whiff of kiwi-scented shampoo. Heather sits next to me, but far enough away that we each have personal space. I look at the computer to see the photos she took, and I'm amazed. I know she's talented but damn! These photos look amazing. She clicks through each one, and it's like a time-lapse through the sun rising.

"These are amazing." I praise her.

"You think so?" She chews on her bottom lip.

"I know so, you should let me see if my boss will put them on the website."

"I don't know…"

"Have you seen the website? It's in need of a major overhaul. We'll be bringing in tons of customers if we have photos like yours on there."

"Are you sure?"

"Uh yeah, you make this place look amazing."

"What about when your boss asks how I got this angle?"

"Let me handle that part," I reassure her.

"Okay." She smiles, nodding.

"Perfect." Now all I have to do is convince my boss not to fire me, but instead reward my new "girlfriend" for taking such amazing photos.

NINE

Heather

"You really don't have to pick me up," I tell Sage over the phone. It's easier to call her than texting back and forth.

"I know, but if it's a date and we want it to look like a date, then I need to pick you up. I would pick you up if this were a real date," she explains.

"Okay." I don't protest; it's not like I can't be driven by her.

"I'll be there in twenty. I just have to make a quick stop first."

"Okay," I say again.

We hang up, and I go back to putting on my mascara. I want to look as good as possible, even if Sage knows it isn't real. This town is small, and we're headed to the park for a picnic together. It's a very public spot to hard launch us as a couple. I put on one of my cutest lavender sundresses, a pair of white Converse, and curl my hair. I swipe some lip gloss across my lips, and I'm ready for our date.

We decided that it would be best to do this in public, then take some photos together and post them on social media. It was essentially a hard launch of our relationship without saying too much. Social media makes it easy for people to know what's going on in our lives. And while I don't follow Jane anymore, she's been a follower I can't seem to get rid of. I don't know if she's just checking in on me or if she actually just forgot to unfollow me. Probably the latter, honestly. But either way, the photos will pop up on her feed, and I can feel somewhat better when we run into each other again.

My phone dings, and a text tells me =Sage is outside. I grab my camera and head out the front door. Sage is leaning against the hood of her car, looking up at the sun, and it does something to my insides. She's dressed in these tight, khaki pants that shape her thighs perfectly and show off how muscular they are. Damn, I wouldn't mind those wrapped around my—focus, Heather! It's been way too long since I hooked up with anyone, but it won't help anyone if I start fantasizing about my fake girlfriend.

She's wearing a black T-shirt that shows off her tattooed arms, and the walk to her car gives me a moment to ogle. Sage is hot, there's no denying that. It'll definitely help make Jane jealous.

"Hey, these are for you." Sage smiles and pulls a bouquet of flowers out from behind her. They're pink roses in full bloom, and they're beautiful.

"For me?" I ask, surprised, taking the flowers.

"Yeah, I know this is all *fake*, but I was taught to never show up to a date without some flowers," she says with a shrug.

"Well thank you, I don't think I've ever gotten flowers before," I admit. I didn't know that was something people still did.

"You're kidding," Sage says, mouth hanging open.

"Nope."

She just shakes her head, walks over to the passenger side of the car, and opens the door for me. I smile and mumble my thanks. I know this is just a fake date, but it isn't lost on me that Sage is pulling out all the stops. Is this really what it's like to be on a date with her? Surely she must just be putting on a show for me.

"Here, I'll put them in the trunk until later. I don't want them to get dried out," Sage says, taking the flowers from me. She closes the car door, and I buckle up.

As she gets in, she turns the volume of the music up a bit and picks up her phone. "You can put on whatever; I just like to drive with music." She hands me her phone, and I'm shocked at the lack of passcode. I don't think Jane ever just handed over her phone so easily. Not that it matters what Sage has on it. I need to remind myself of that fact. This is all pretend.

"Anything you *don't* like?" I ask before scrolling through Spotify.

"I hate country and EDM, but otherwise, I'm totally open."

"Okay." That gives me enough wiggle room. I go to her liked artists to find someone familiar to play. I smile when I see several of my favorite artists here too. I finally settle on the newest Fletcher song and press play.

"Oh! This one is so good!" Sage nods and turns up the music again.

"It's one of my favorites." I smile.

"I love her first album, I saw her live in New York when I was still living there. Let me just say, she's just as beautiful and talented in person." Sage gushes.

"Ah, I'm so jealous. She's on my bucket list of tours."

"Who else is on this list?"

"Oh, well…Harry Styles, Halsey, and Olivia Rodrigo—just to name a few."

"I've seen Halsey. So fucking good. Harry's on mine, too, but I'm not an Olivia Rodrigo fan past 'Driver's License,'" Sage admits.

"I get that. I really think both her albums are amazing."

Sage starts humming along as another Fletcher song comes on, and I decide to leave it. It sounds good, and the drive isn't too much longer.

"So, we didn't really talk much about this. But um, you're not, like… seeing anyone else, right? It's okay if you are, but I just don't want to be caught up and people see you with someone else—"

"Hey, no worries. I'm not seeing anyone else. So, we're good." She pauses. "I'm assuming the same goes for you."

"Oh, yeah. I told you, I'm nowhere near ready for a relationship," I say and it's true. As much as I think about one, I still need time to get over things.

"We're here," Sage says as she pulls into a spot at the end of the parking lot. She unlocks the trunk, taking out a reusable shopping bag, and I follow her.

"What did you pack?" I ask curiously. She assured me not to eat and that she would take care of everything. It's one of the first times I'm trusting someone to make decisions about my meals. Of course, I have an extra protein bar and applesauce pouch in my purse just in case.

"Peanut butter and jelly sandwiches, apples, and potato chips. I also made some chocolate chip cookies." She smiles.

"I can't remember the last time I had a PB&J." I smile.

"Same, but it was something vegan so I thought it was a safe option." She chuckles. "How about here?" She points to the spot under the shady tree.

"Looks great." I smile.

Sage pulls out a white sheet and puts it on the ground then takes a seat against the tree. She pulls the bag onto the middle of the sheet, and I take a seat across from her. I'm careful to cross my legs and make sure I don't accidentally flash her my thong. She hands me a wrapped sandwich and pulls out two bottles of iced tea.

"This is so good." I moan into my sandwich. It brings me back to elementary school when I'd come home from school and have one as an afternoon snack.

"I'll have to get a list of more foods you like that are vegan so I can be more prepared for our next date." Sage winks and my stomach does this weird flutter thing. I mentally tell my stomach to knock it off—she means *fake* date.

"I eat basically all the fruits, veggies, nuts, and the fake dairy products." I shrug and pop and apple slice in my mouth.

"Gotcha, so we'd be able to go to a restaurant then?"

"Yes, Sage. I do go to restaurants." I laugh.

"I like the way you say my name." She smiles. Her eyes linger just a little bit too long on my lips, and I don't know if she's faking it, or she's that good of an actress.

"Watch out!" a boy screams just as a football comes hurtling our way. At the last second, Sage kicks it out of the way from hitting me in the face.

"Shit." I breathe.

"That was close!" the other boy yells.

"Next time, hit it over that way please?" Sage smiles and hands the kids back the ball. "Are you alright?"

"Yeah, you uh, saved me. Those were some quick reflexes," I say, impressed.

"I didn't want that pretty little face to get damaged." Sage winks and my stomach goes to mush. *Traitor.* She is definitely flirting with me, but that's allowed, right? I don't know I'm supposed to act with a fake girlfriend when you're in public but no one can hear you.

"We should take some photos while the lighting is still nice," I decide.

"Sure." She nods.

I pause—it *would* be cute to get the background of the tree and the park in the photo. So I stand, sit down closer to Sage, and pick up my camera. She looks nervous, so I sit a little closer to her and she seems to tense up. Am I making her nervous?

"Relax, it's supposed to look natural." I smile and put a hand on her thigh. It's a friendly gesture, but I'm instantly hit with a thousand volts of electricity through my fingers. I don't move them, determined to move past whatever this is that's going on with me.

"Oh, you have a leaf in your hair." She turns toward me, brushes my bangs from my forehead and takes a strand of pink hair between her fingertips—which I notice are manicured but cut as short as can be. I blush as she takes the leaf out and tucks the piece of hair back behind my ear. I don't realize I'm staring at her until she looks at me expectantly.

"Should we smile?" she asks, clearing her throat.

"Uh, sure." I nod and shake my head to clear my thoughts. What is up with me today? I feel like my cheeks are on fire, and I can't stop noticing things about Sage—things that aren't like me to notice.

I force a smile, flip the camera up to take a photo of us, and *click.* As I go to take another one, Sage wraps her arm around my shoulders and pulls me in slightly. I'm sure she's just doing it for the photos, but she smells so good; it's like some kind of body spray, and I'm intoxicated by the scent. Sage's arm is still around me while I smile, and we get a few where we're looking at each other.

"Is that good?" Sage pulls back her arm, and I can breathe clearly again.

"I'm sure they are. I'll edit them tonight and send you one to post," I say. I take my seat back across from her and nibble on the apple slices. I need to get these thoughts of Sage—and whatever my body is doing around her—out of my head. I can't be having feelings for my fake girlfriend, especially not now. I'm sure this is just a platonic crush I'm having, and it'll be gone soon.

"When you're done eating, want to take a walk down by the water?" Sage suggests.

My heart does a flip at the thought of it. But I quickly shut it down. I can't do this. Suddenly, I'm remembering how bad it felt to get my heart broken by Jane. I'm not ready for anything more than what Sage and I have. I can't afford to get hurt again.

"I'd love to, but I'm sort of chilly. Maybe another time?" I smile and rub my shoulders for good measure. Sage's face falls slightly but she nods, understanding.

TEN

Sage

———

"When were you going to tell me you have a girlfriend?!" Maeve squeals over the phone.

"Maeve..." I start but I'm cut off by more squealing.

"I can't believe it. I thought you didn't have time to date and here you are making it official right away like some true lesbian," she teases.

"There's something I have to tell you." I sigh.

"What?" She quiets and I take a deep breath. I start explaining what the hell is going on between Heather and I, and the fact that it's nothing to be actually excited about.

"Oh." I picture her face falling.

"It sucks because I'm starting to like her for real, but she's made it super clear she's not ready for a relationship right now." I sigh and slump into my bed.

"It's possible that could change, just a few weeks ago you didn't even want to consider the option of dating anyone, and now here you are liking someone."

"Maybe." I doubt it. She was so clear about it, and I don't want her to feel pressured in any way.

"What are you up to today then?" Maeve asks.

"I was supposed to study for this big test, but there's someone working on their house today, and I can't focus. I was actually calling to see if you wanted to get together and study."

"Oh, I wish I could but my brother is in town, and I said I'd take him to lunch. Raincheck?"

"Of course. Have fun with him."

We hang up and I lie back on the bed, grumbling. Of course, at this exact moment, a jackhammer starts outside my window and you can't hear anything else. Grumbling, I grab my stuff and head outside. Maybe I can get some work done at Love in a Cup; it shouldn't be too crowded today. But as I pull into the parking lot, I'm less than hopeful. It takes me three times of driving in circles to find a parking spot fifteen minutes away. By the time I get inside, there's a line almost out the door. What the hell? Are they giving away free coffee or something?

"Sorry, there's an event going on today, we're only doing to-go orders," the barista explains and points to the sign in front of her. I sigh and order a coffee anyway. At least I'll be caffeinated— even though I don't have anywhere to study.

"Sage?" a familiar voice calls out while I sugar my coffee.

"Heather?" I look up and see my fake girlfriend in line for coffee.

"What are you doing here?" she asks as I walk over to her.

"I was hoping to study here, but I didn't know they were hosting an event." I frown.

"You can't study at home?"

"They're doing work on my neighbor's house. It's literally right outside my window."

"Ah, I'm sorry." She pauses. "Why don't you come over?"

"Really?"

"Yeah, I have the space, and I'm just editing wedding photos today. I was just taking a break to get a drink." She smiles.

"Okay, if you're sure I'm not imposing."

"Not at all, I'm happy to have you," Heather reassures me. She's called next, orders her iced matcha tea, and I step in to pay for her.

"What?" She looks at me, confused.

"It's the least I can do, babe," I say with a wink. I doubt she knows anyone here, but it doesn't hurt to play the girlfriend role just in case.

"Th-thanks." is that a blush I creeping up on her cheeks?

She grabs her tea and turns to me. "I'll meet you at the house then?"

"Sounds good." I smile. What are the odds? I'm so glad I thought to take a chance on the coffee shop today.

Driving over to Heather's place is quick, and I actually make it there before her by some miracle. So I wait in the car, and five minutes later, Heather pulls up next to me. Sliding her shades on the top of her head, she waves me over and I follow her into the house.

"Make yourself at home. I'm going to grab my laptop." She motions to the house.

"Do you have a table I can sit at? I don't wanna get too comfortable on the couch."

"Oh yeah, dining room is straight through there." She points and I follow to an oversized white and pale-blue dining room. The table is large enough to seat eight, and I wonder how big her friend's family is. Taking a seat at the head of the table, I move the placemat out of the way and pull out my textbook, notebook, pens, highlighters and laptop.

"Wow you come prepared." Heather chuckles.

"It's an important test. I could fail the class if I don't pass," I explain.

"Shit, well I'll be sure not to distract you then." She motions the zipping of her lips and takes a seat next to me.

Heather is tapping away on the laptop in front of her, clearly in editing mode, so I dive in. It's for my social work class, so it's a lot of memorizing terms. Part of the test will be in multiple choice, but the second half will be short answer. I pull out the practice test she gave us, and I write down my answers on a spare sheet of paper so I can retake it when I'm done. I'm halfway through the test when I look up because I can feel Heather's eyes on me.

"What?" I ask.

"Oh nothing, sorry. I was just daydreaming." She looks back at her laptop, and I raise an eyebrow but don't push it further.

I try to go back to my test, but now it's me who's staring at Heather. She's got her hair pulled into a messy bun on the top of her head today with her bangs clipped back. I don't think she's wearing any makeup, and it's the first time I've seen her in a T-shirt. She looks relaxed compared to the last time I saw her. She has her knee up on the chair and is resting her chin on it while she works. It makes me think about that joke Maeve always says; you can always spot a bisexual by the way they sit in chairs. Most of the time, that's right.

Attempting to focus, I take a sip of my coffee and look back at my test. Finishing it, I go over it with the answer key my professor provided and realize I got a ninety-six. For the first time, I consider stopping there. I mean, ninety-six percent is enough to pass the class and keep my scholarship. Do I really need to get a perfect score on everything?

"I'm going to make some lunch, would you like some?" Heather asks, standing up.

"Oh, I don't need anything, but thanks," I lie. My stomach is grumbling, but I'm sure I have some protein bars in my bag somewhere.

"Okay, I'll make extra just in case," she says with a shrug.

The kitchen is just off the dining room so I can see her in the corner of my eye as she flitters around the kitchen looking for things. She grabs a large bowl, a cutting board, and a variety of ingredients from the fridge. Heather starts chopping up some broccoli and boiling water on the stove. I try not to stare, but I'm curious about what she's making.

"Do you need any help?" I ask.

"Nah, but thanks." She waves me off with a knife.

I decide to retake my test, just in case. This time it's harder to focus when I see Heather bending to pick up some of the broccoli she dropped. Her ass is in the air for enough time for me to look and then act like I wasn't looking. Damn, she was hot in every angle. It wasn't helping how attracted to her I was. She was just so beautiful and easy to be around. I felt like I had been friends with her for forever and there was an ease about us. I wondered if she felt the same.

Heather comes back to the table holding two bowls and places one in front of me. "It's creamy vegan pasta with broccoli. Mine has tofu, but I left it out in yours."

"Oh, thank you. You didn't—"

"It's my pleasure." She cuts me off with a grin.

I take a bite and I'm surprised to find it's actually really good. "Wow, this is good," I say aloud.

"You sound surprised." She laughs.

"I didn't know vegan food could taste this good," I admit.

"It's not all raw veggies and tofu, you just have to know how to cook."

I finish the bowl, and Heather takes both bowls to the sink.

"Would you want to work outside for a bit? It's not so hot anymore, and the view is nice out there," Heather suggests.

"Sure." I nod. Gathering my things, I follow her out the patio doors. There's a glass table with a huge white umbrella in the middle. Heather takes one of the chairs out and sits down, so I sit across from her.

"I like to come out here and think sometimes; it's so peaceful. It's been too hot during the day lately."

"I hate the heat," I admit.

"Me too, unless I'm at the beach, I do not want to be a thousand degrees." She shakes her head.

"How are your edits coming along?"

"Good, I'm almost done. I just need to finish this last chunk, and then I can update the clients folder and my website," she explains. "How's studying?"

"Slow." I chuckle. "I know the information. I'm just afraid I'll forget it before the test or something."

"How would you forget it if you know it?"

"I don't know. But that's what I worry about." I shrug.

Heather nods and we go back to silently working. She's clacking away on her computer, and I'm re-reading the chapters in the text-book that are on the test. I stretch my legs out to get a little more comfortable, and I accidentally knock a foot into her calf.

"Sorry," I mumble, but she just smiles.

I go to move my legs into a comfortable but safe spot and leave them. But a moment later, Heather's foot is touching mine. I glance up at her, but she's too deep in her work to notice. I guess that was nothing. But then she starts moving her foot, ever so slightly like she's trying to play footsie with me or something. I don't move, frozen and unsure of how to proceed. I glance up at her, but she's still working away. She doesn't move for a moment, and then once again, she moves her foot against mine. She's definitely playing footsie now. So I do what any normal person with a crush would do, and I play footsie back. I'm almost thirty years old, but I'm playing footsie with the woman I like. I try to focus on my textbook while I do, but I'm not the best multitasker, and this is taking a lot out of me.

Suddenly, Heather giggles. "Are we really playing footsie, right now?"

"Hey, you started it." I laugh.

"Well, someone knocked into me first," she teases.

I push back lightly on her foot one last time, and she does the same. I just laugh, as she chews on her bottom lip. I can tell she's holding something back, but I don't know what it is. Is she flirting with me or is this all this is? A stupid game of footsie between adults? She goes back to her work, but her foot rests on mine and I don't move an inch. Even when my foot falls asleep and all I feel are pins and needles, I don't twitch. This crush is going to kill me, but I'll be damned if I move.

ELEVEN

Heather

"You two playing footsie?!" my sister teases over the phone. I need to vent to someone about what's going on. Considering my sister is states away and has always been my vault, I know I can trust her.

"I mean, yes." I blush even thinking about it. I don't think I've ever even played footsie before the other night.

"So you like her, then?" she guesses.

"What? How did you get that from footsie?"

"It's like low-key flirting. A way that's not so obvious but also obvious at the same time."

"Hmm." I don't know what to say.

"You can like her you know, even if you're just faking the relationship."

"No. It's way too soon." I shake my head.

"It's been months HJ; if you need more time to heal that's totally okay. But it's also okay for you to move on. Jane is and she didn't even wait until you guys broke up," she points out. I know she's not trying to hurt me by saying this, but it still stings.

"I-I just can't yet." I don't elaborate. But I just know I can't date anyone right now. I'm not ready, and it wouldn't be fair to Sage or anyone else if I tried.

"Okay. But do you maybe like her? Even if it's just a little?"

"A little," I admit. It's hard not to. Once you get past her looks, her personality is just as hot. She's funny and thoughtful, and she seems to be happy no matter what we do. We sit in silence for hours while I'm editing, and she's studying and she seems happy just to be there. There isn't anything complicated about Sage and being with her.

"I'm just saying, maybe see how it goes. You don't have to act on it, but if you did happen to fall for her, from what you told me, it seems likely that she'd like you too."

"Okay." I sigh, this wasn't the conversation I expected to have with her when I started this phone call.

"Hey, let me go Clara just got home, and I want to see how her audition went."

"Of course, tell her hello from me. Love ya." I blow a kiss and she ends the call.

Sage is due to come over any minute. We have a pending date for another public outing, but honestly, that's the last thing I want to do today. I'm not in the mood to put on a show for anyone, but I don't want to cancel either. Maybe Sage wouldn't mind just watching a movie or something. We could make popcorn and cuddle—I mean sit on the couch a good distance apart. What's up with me lately? I don't have time to unpack that one.

"Heather?" Sage calls out, and I jump from my bed. Without time to check if I have bedhead, I run to the front door to let her in.

"Hey Sage." I smile. Something about seeing her makes my heart flutter a bit.

"Are you ready to go?"

"Uh, actually do you think we could raincheck? I don't really feel like going out tonight."

Sage's disappointment is written all over her face. "Of course, no worries. I'll see you—"

"You can stay!" I say a little too excitedly. "I mean..." I get myself under control. "You can stay."

"Oh, cool." Sage nods and slips off her sneakers by the door and comes in.

"I thought we could watch a movie? I have popcorn."

"Sounds good to me." Sage smiles.

"I'll be right back. The remote is on the table; you can put Netflix on, and we can choose something together."

"Okay." She walks in as I walk into the kitchen.

Suddenly, I feel more nervous than I did before. This feels more date-like than all the other times she's been over. I know it isn't, I mean, it can't be a date if only one of you thinks it is. But still, my palms are sweaty, and I can feel my heart racing. I try to distract myself while I put the popcorn in the microwave. I grab two glasses for water and a bowl for the popcorn. We can share, right? Yeah, that's what normal people do. I try to convince myself this is just two friends watching a movie together. Who cares if we're fake girl-friends? When we're alone, we're just friends, right?

Pop! Pop! Pop!

The popcorn beeps, and I carefully pour it into the bowl. Carrying everything out in one trip takes some maneuvering, but I manage. Placing everything on the table, I notice Sage is in my seat. Not that I claimed it or anything, but it just happens to be where I spend most nights. Instead of saying anything, I just take a seat next to her, making sure to leave a normal amount of friend-distance as I look at the TV. Netflix's home page blinks at us, waiting for us to pick something.

"What kind of movies do you like?" I ask.

"Anything really, maybe not horror tonight though, since I have to drive home," she says with a light chuckle.

"Gotcha, scaredy cat," I tease with a wink, and she pushes my arm playfully. The feeling of her fingers lingers on my skin while I try to remind myself we're just friends.

"How about a classic?" she says scrolling through the pages.

"What?"

"*The Notebook*? It's incredibly outdated and they probably

shouldn't have been together, but it's a great movie even if the couple is straight."

I crack a smile. "I love this movie."

"Oh shit, I'm sorry—"

"No, you're right. It's a comfort movie; my mom always liked it when I was growing up. But you're totally right. They fight like crazy, and we're told love is enough for them. I'd love to watch it though."

"I might have some opinions about it."

"Bring them," I say with a smile.

Sage turns on the movie, and since it's already dark in the room, I lean back into the couch. I put the bowl of popcorn between us and take a handful to toss into my mouth. The movie starts just as I remember, and I smile, remembering how I would always ask my mom to watch it with her. She loves her movies. When I was at my parents the other day she had a movie playing in the background. I can't think of what it was now, but it was definitely a romance. My mom loves her romances. Plus, she lived one with my dad, being married for over thirty years.

I'm watching Noah and Allie kiss, and a thought pops into my head. What would it feel like to kiss Sage? Would she be sweet and tender, or would she be a little aggressive and bite my lip? I shiver at the thought. She has these slender pink lips that look more kissable lately. I sneak a glance at her while I reach for a new handful of popcorn, and she smiles at me. I blush…

If only she knew what I'm thinking.

What if I got her to kiss me? Maybe then my feelings and thoughts about her would disappear. But how could I casually ask her to kiss me without it being weird? I don't want our new friendship to change or to make our fake romance change. Oh my gosh. That's it! I could tell her it's practice for our fake relationship! She has to believe that, doesn't she? I mean, it sounds plausible to me. A little kiss just to make our relationship look real. We don't want to be caught off guard if someone questions us. We'll look like idiots if our first kiss is in front of everyone and we somehow missed or something.

Now it's a matter of asking her. I just need to put my big girl panties and ask her. It

It's no big deal, something casual. She doesn't even have to say yes. Although, that would be an ego hit for sure, I could handle it. I don't want to push her into anything either. I reach for the popcorn again, ready to stuff my face, when I catch Sage's hand in the bowl.

"Oh! Sorry!" we both mumble and pull our hands out. I blush. We only touched fingertips, and I'm blushing. How could I handle kissing her? No, I need to do this. I *can* do this.

But instead of saying anything, I turn my attention back to the movie. I watch Noah and Allie fall in love and ignore the butterflies in my stomach at the thought of asking Sage to kiss me.

"Hey, so I've been thinking about something…" I say quietly.

"What's up?" Sage looks at me raising an eyebrow, as if to ask if she should be worried.

"So we don't have to, but I was thinking, just in case it comes up, or really just to make it more believable, maybe we should kiss. You know, at least once so we won't be caught off guard if and when it happens in public." When I'm done, I unclench my eyelids and glance Sage's way. She's smirking and I can't tell what she's thinking.

"Heather, are you asking me to kiss you? For *practice*?"

"Well, I just thought we should be prepared for anything. But if you don't want to…"

"You're joking right? Why wouldn't I want to? You're beautiful," Sage says as if it's obvious. My heart flutters, and I try to remember to breathe. This is actually happening.

"Thanks," I mutter quietly.

"Can I kiss you right now? Or is this like a planned practice in the future?" she asks.

"Now is cool, or whenever." I add a shrug and hope I sound extra casual, but I'm sure my face is darker than my hair, and my lack of eye contact is making it obvious.

"Come here." Sage brushes her fingers up my arm. I twist to move closer to her, accidentally knocking over the remaining bowl of popcorn.

"Ignore it," Sage says in a commanding tone, so I nod and move closer to her. I'm sitting on popcorn but I don't care. *Sage* was about to kiss me.

"You're sure about this?" She checks as she pushes a piece of my hair behind my ear.

"I'm sure." I nod.

Closing my eyes, I lean forward ever so slightly, and her lips connect with mine. Lips as soft as I imagined, pressing against my own. And just as quickly as it starts, it's over. Sage pulls back and smiles.

"How was that?"

"That was…" I pause. "It was good, but maybe we should try it again? A little more this time? If you want," I quickly add and she laughs.

Instead of speaking, she runs her hand over my cheek, brushes it into the side of my hair, and leans in to kiss me. Her lips press against mine softly once more, but this time she slips her tongue lightly into my mouth. I let my tongue follow her lead. The longer we kiss, the more heated it becomes. What begins as a subtle kiss, turns eagerly into a casual but sultry make out. Sage's tongue is like fire, and mine is the embers keeping it burning. I don't hold back my moan when she sucks gently on my tongue. *Fuck.* That went straight to my panties.

We pull apart for a second to take a breath, but almost instantly, we're ravenous for each other all over again. It's like the last several weeks of sexual tension and chemistry have been building up to this moment. Sage somehow does this move where she scoops me onto her lap. I gasp, realizing I'm basically straddling her in nothing but a pair of short shorts and an old T-shirt. I didn't even remember to put on a bra today.

My chest leans against hers, and she's the one to moan this time as I run my fingers through her short hair. Soft as her skin, I make a mental note to ask what kind of conditioner she uses later. I tug lightly on her hair, and she nips at my bottom lip. Her tongue is back in my mouth just as quick but her hands are sliding down the arch of my back and land on my ass. She takes one cheek in each hand and grabs on tight. I grind slightly on her lap, my pussy growing wetter by the second with each move.

My hands move down Sage's neck and toward the front of her. I brush my hands over her chest, and I can feel her pebbled nibbles through her shirt and what I make out to be a sports bra. She was as turned on as I was. I hadn't meant for it to go this far, but now that we started, I don't want to stop. Thankfully, Sage seems to have more restraint then me.

"I-I think we should stop." She pulls away and looks at me with doe eyes. I can tell she's saying the opposite of how she's feeling. But she's right. We don't want to take this too far.

"You're right." I nod. I go to slide off her lap but she stops me at the last second, uttering something that sounds like "fuck it" under her breath.

Sage pulls me back into her lap and kisses me fiercely before letting me go. Lightheaded, I slip onto the couch next to her. The only sounds are us clearly out of breath and the movie still playing in the background.

"That the kinda practice you had in mind?" Sage asks with a smirk. Instead of answering, I throw a pillow at her head. We both burst out laughing, which leads to a pillow fight of epic proportions. Who knew Alana's family had so many pillows?

I don't think I've ever used my vibrator as many times as I have in the past week. I most definitely got my money's worth. I'm actually afraid it might crap out and die on me after using it three times today. But damn, I'm incredibly pent up from the make out session at Heather's house. I know we probably could've gone further, and I wouldn't be in this situation. What's the female equivalent of blue balls? Because whatever it is, I have it.

When Heather asked to kiss me, I was shocked. But I would've been an idiot to say no. I know it'll probably make things confusing in the long run, like after the wedding when we don't have to pretend anymore. But until then, I have no probably kissing my fake girlfriend like she's my real girlfriend. I'll show her exactly what she'd be getting if this were all real.

That's why, before our date today, I stop to pick up a bouquet of flowers for her. It's another set of pink flowers to match her hair—but this time, it's carnations. My mom always told me one of the things my father did before he left us was bring her flowers. He'd bring them before every date and anytime he was seeing her, no matter the occasion or lack thereof. Despite him not sticking around after she told him she was expecting me, I love the flowers idea, so

I've made it a tradition. Heather and I are only going swimming by the lighthouse today, but I still want to make sure she had a fresh bouquet.

"Sage! I'm over here!" Heather calls my name, and I have to stop my jaw from hanging open.

Heather is wearing a pink bikini that I'm pretty sure has less coverage than my normal underwear. Her breasts are perfectly round, fitting inside the strapless top, while her ass is basically fully exposed. She's wearing a thin pair of matching bottoms, but they go up the curve of her ass almost like a thong. I swallow hard. Today is going to be difficult. Heather looks hot on a normal day with clothes that cover all of her. But today? I wish I had packed a darker pair of sunglasses. Clearly by the time I get home I'll be needing to use my vibrator again.

"Hey." I smile as I reach her in the sand.

"I'm glad you're here. Is this spot okay? I don't like to be too close to the water because then the kids splash me," she explains and motions toward her stuff. It consists of a long beach towel, a low white chair, and a beach cooler.

"Yeah, here's cool." I drop the chair I'm holding next to hers and place my stuff next to it. "These are for you." I smile and hand her the bouquet.

"Wow! I love these, thanks." Her reaction is bigger than last time, but I also remind myself that we're outside. There's more people around which means a bigger audience.

"Anything for my girl." I lean in and kiss the back of her hair. It's still dry, which means she hasn't gone in the water yet.

"It's a beautiful day," she says changing the subject.

"Did you wanna go for a dip? I'm sweating," I admit.

"Sure, do you need sunscreen?"

"Nah, I put some on at home. How about you?" I take the opportunity to glance over her body again. Damn, I want to commit this to memory.

"I put some on before you came." She smiles.

I take off my T-shirt, exposing a bathing suit sports bra, and kick off my flip flops. We both walk past a bunch of families to get to the water. Once we're there, we dive right in. I'm relieved to be in the cool water instead of the hot sun. I was sweltering just on the walk from my car to the sand.

"How did you do on your test?" Heather asks, smiling. I'm surprised she remembered; I don't know if I even told her when it was.

"It was great, I got a 100," I say proudly.

"Wow! That's awesome."

"Did the clients like the wedding photos?"

"Oh yes! And the engagement shoot is this week, so I'm excited for it. The groom-to-be is SO nervous it's actually kind of cute."

"I can imagine. I mean, what if she says no?"

"Well, you shouldn't ask someone if you don't know that they'll say yes," she points out.

"True." I nod.

We swim around for a bit in the deeper water, then move over to the rocky shore. Sitting on one of the oversized rocks, we're covered by the shade of some of the trees nearby. We're both kicking our feet in the water when Heather splashes me with her foot.

"Hey!" I yell and splash her back.

Instead of splashing me back, she pushes me into the water, and I pull her in with me. We're both yelling and splashing each other—until Heather comes closer to me and I grab her wrist. I'm about to tell her not to splash me again when she bites on her bottom lip. I don't know what comes over me, but it can only be described as lust. I pull her into me, push my lips against hers, and slip my tongue in her mouth.

My back is against the rocks while Heather wraps her legs against my body. We kiss like we're hungry for each other, desperate for more. Her lips never leave mine, so I grip her ass as she's wrapped around me. I'm grateful for this bathing suit that leaves very little to the imagination. She brushes a hand against my chest, and I moan, my nipples sensitive to her touch. I want to do more, explore her, but it wasn't the right time. Or the place for that matter. When I finally had my way with Heather, it's going to be in a bed…

And she'll be more than just my *fake* girlfriend.

"What kind of conditioner do you use?" Heather asks randomly. We're sitting on the chairs, beachside after our little make out.

"I'm sorry, what?" I look at her, confused.

"Uh, your hair is really soft. So I was wondering what kind of conditioner you use." She blushes.

"When did you—OH." I was about to ask when she felt my hair, but my mind slips back to the other night. Was she just thinking about that night? Is that why that popped into her head?

"I believe I use Pantene, but it's nothing special." I wink.

"Cool, cool." She looks away, and I can tell she's embarrassed.

I couldn't blame her for thinking about it. I've been replaying the last few minutes in my head. Thinking about kissing her is all I can do until the next chance I have to kiss her. We haven't really talked about what it means—if anything. But I figure today is part of the "in public" PDA we have to "practice" for.

"Have you been able to find an apartment?" I ask as I pop a Lactaid pill in my mouth. I hate being lactose intolerant, but I hate the side effects more. So I chew the white pill, then wash it down with a handful of Cheetos.

"Not yet. It seems like everything is being used for the summer, so a lot of places told me to check back in the fall."

"I'm sorry."

"It's okay. Alana doesn't mind me staying, and honestly, it's like living at my own bed and breakfast. The place is amazing."

"It is," I agree.

"I just realized I've never seen your apartment."

"Yeah, that's true." I shrug. "It's nothing special."

"Can I see it anyway?" She looks at me over her sunglasses. Her big, blue eyes, begging.

"Yeah, sure."

"Like now?"

"Now?"

"Why not? I'm done swimming. We could check it out and order in some food or just go out to eat after." She smiles.

"Okay," I say after thinking about it. Hopefully I remembered to pick up my dirty laundry from the corner of my room.

We start to pack up our things and head toward the parking lot.

"Do you want to follow me, or should I text you the address?"

"I can follow you." Heather smiles.

"Okay, see you soon."

I'm not nervous on the way to my apartment; it's not like Heather and I have never been alone before. And for an apartment, mine is pretty nice. It's much smaller than the beach house she was staying at, but I don't think she'll care about something like that. I check my rearview mirror and see Heather's car behind me. I turn onto my street and hope there's parking for her. It's the middle of the day, so thankfully, not everyone's home yet and she finds a spot on the corner. I open the front door and Heather follows behind me.

"You don't have any roommates? I guess you would've mentioned already if you did."

"Yeah, I don't." I shake my head.

Heather looks around curiously, but my eyes are on her. She's wearing a beach cover-up that covers nothing. It's white, basically transparent since her bathing suit was wet, and it hangs just to the top of her thighs. With each step she takes, it moves with her, showing another inch of her ass.

"You play video games?" she asks looking at my bookshelf in the living room.

"Yeah,. I hang my head. "Mostly my Nintendo Switch."

"That's cool. I want one but I don't know if I'd actually play it," she says with a light shrug.

"Is that your bedroom?" She peeks at the half open door, and I nod.

"You can look around. I'm pretty sure it's not the cleanest though," I admit and rub the back of my neck.

"Please, you've never seen a place I've lived in yet. My bedroom at the house is a mess." Heather laughs. She pushes my bedroom door open, and I hang back, leaning on the door frame of the bedroom.

Heather looks around, first at the posters over my TV. They are mainly indie bands I like and have seen in concert. My dresser drawers are actually closed with no clothes poking out. But she stops short at the bed, and I see it at the same time. In the middle of my unmade bed, is my bright pink vibrator. My very obvious, life-like vibrator. I'm pretty sure I try to combust in this moment but nothing happens. Heather is silent, and I feel like years pass before she speaks.

"I have the old model of this; how's this one's speed?" Heather holds it up like we're talking about shoe sizes or what food to order for dinner and not a sex toy. I don't know whether to be turned on or embarrassed at her statement.

"I-it um. It works great. Very…um. Fast," I manage to choke out.

"Hmm." She holds it up and I'm thankful I at least washed it after the many times I used it last night— and this morning.

"You can, uh, try it out if you want." I don't mean it the way it sounds. "I meant the speeds—" I'm cut off by the sound of dull vibrations circulating the room.

I swallow hard. Heather is not only touching my vibrator, but she's checking to see how fast it can go? In the palm of her small hands, the toy looks huge. I can't help but wonder how it would look in other places. I'm wet just thinking about it. This whole moment is etched into my mind for later.

"Seems like it would get the job done." She turns it off and tosses it back on the bed like it was nothing. I can't will myself to move or even speak.

"Cat got your tongue?" she teases and walks closer to me, chewing on her bottom lip.

"More like hot girl has my vibrator," I manage.

"I'll have to make sure to order that one; it seems fun. But I think you'd know all about that right?" She smirks. And in this moment, I *know* she's teasing me. She *has* to be teasing me. There's no other explanation for it.

THIRTEEN

Heather

When I get back to my place, I grab my own purple vibrator and head for the shower. I don't know how many times I manage to orgasm, but I don't get out until the water runs cold—which gives me the cold shower I so desperately need.

After seeing the vibrator on Sage's bed, I couldn't help myself but tease her. Sometimes it's cute to see how composed she tries to stay. But in reality, I'm thinking about sleeping with her just as much as she's thinking about it. I could see it in her eyes, they were all over me today. I don't blame her; every time we touch it feels like the sparks are literally going to set us on fire.

We've definitely crossed many lines and probably some boundaries, but neither of us brought it up. I don't know what it means for us, but I like wherever it's headed. It feels simple—carefree. I don't have as much at risk this way. I've never been one for just hooking-up, but maybe that's what I need. Hooking-up with Sage wouldn't just be a random hookup; it would be *more*.

I pull out my outfit for tomorrow. We're just grabbing ice cream at the place just outside of town. I've been craving their vegan mint chip , and she said she's always down for ice cream. My strawberry romper is one of my favorite outfits. It'd something I like to wear on first dates. I haven't worn it with Sage. It's low-cut in the front to show-off the gals but short enough to show-off my legs too.

After brushing my hair, I put on a face mask before bed and slip into an oversized T-shirt. I hate sleeping in pants, let alone panties. My girl needs to breathe. My phone buzzes, and I see a text from Sage.

SAGE:

Thinking about you…

ME:

Oh yeah?

SAGE:

Someone was in my room and touching my things today

ME:

Oh no! Who'd do that??

SAGE:

Just this hottie. Made it hard to be in the same room today.

SAGE:

Good thing I'm alone now…

My hands hover over the keyboard on my phone. *Is Sage attempting to sext me?* We've never done that before, but it's not like I'm not curious. I don't want to assume anything, so I let her take the lead.

ME:

Me too…

SAGE:

Can I see you?

.   .   .

I blush. I don't know if I'm ready to send a fully naked photo. So I open the camera, put up a peace sign and send a quick selfie.

SAGE:

Beautiful

ME:

Can I see you?

I almost drop my phone out of my hand when the photo comes through. The view is from above. Sage is lying in bed with just a sports bra on. She looks fucking hot. Her abs are on full display, which I can say are even better in person.

ME:

Damn

SAGE:

Thinking about earlier...

ME:

Tell me more.

If she wants this, I'm going to make her work for it.

SAGE:

I got to make out with the hottest girl.

ME:

Funny, that's what I did today, too.

SAGE:

Made me so turned on…

ME:

Me 2

SAGE:

Whatcha' gunna do about that?

ME:

Who says I'm not doing anything? 😈

I slide my hand down my chest, past my stomach, and to the top of my pussy. I'm freshly waxed and soaking, my fingers sliding down my center. I moan audibly, thankful to be alone in this big house.

SAGE:

TELL ME MORE

I think about sending something, but instead I slide up my shirt, snap a quick picture of my breasts, and send it through. After all, a picture is worth a thousand words.

SAGE:

Fuck.

I need you.

What would you let me do?

ME:

Take it slow first, but then I'd let you taste me...

I'd want to feel how you kiss me down there.

SAGE:

I've been dying for a taste.

ME:

I want to ride your face.

I send it before I can overthink it, but it's something I've been thinking about since our first make out on the couch. Climbing her like a tree and letting her eat me out until I'm screaming sounds like an absolute dream.

SAGE:

I'd love to have you wrapped around my face.

ME:

I'll use your toy on you when you're done.

SAGE:

Fuck. I'm using it right now, but I only want you.

ME:

Just think about me touching you, your nipples in my mouth and how close I am to coming.

SAGE:

Show me?

If you want...

I pause. I'm not against sending nudes—videos or otherwise. So I pull back the blankets, open the camera app, and take a video of my fingers sliding up and down my pussy. I press *send* and wait for the parade of texts I know I'm going to get. But instead of texts, I get an incoming FaceTime call. I hesitate for a second, but then click answer.

"Hello?" I only show my face in the video.

"Holy fuck, that was so hot." Sage's voice is deep with desire.

"Glad you liked it." I chew on my bottom lip.

"I hope it's okay I called, I thought maybe it would be easier than texting?"

"Yeah, I like this idea." I nod.

"So, please continue." Sage motions and I slide my shirt back up my chest, exposing my breasts.

"Damn." Sage moans and I can hear the sound of her vibrator clicking on.

"If you're going to touch yourself, you at least need to show the class," I tease.

"Yes ma'am." She moves the phone away from her face and shows that despite wearing a sports bra, she's completely bare on the bottom. The sight of her pussy is hot as fuck. She's got a cute little landing strip down the center but otherwise, she's bare.

"Mmm," I groan and move the phone so she can see my other hand has returned to my pussy.

"Oh, god. You have the prettiest pussy." Sage moans and I watch as she pushes the toy in and out of her pussy. I watch as she turns up the vibration, and I start to rub small circles across my clit.

"Fuck, you're dripping baby. Is that all for me?" I love the way she calls me baby. It's like fire to the flame.

"Yes." I gasp. "I want you."

"What I wouldn't do to touch you right now." She groans.

"I'm so wet, and I already came a few times when I got home," I admit.

"You did? Fuck."

"I was so turned on after leaving your place."

"I wish I would've known."

There's an unspoken silence between us about not saying

anything too real out loud. This is in the moment and not anything more or anything less than right now.

"I want to see you come for me."

"Yeah? Only if you come with me."

"Deal," I say, smirking.

For the next few minutes, there's nothing but moans and gasping while we both watch each other. I'm close, but I don't want to come without her. Watching Sage touch herself while thinking about me is more than enough to get me close.

"I'm, fuck—I'm coming!" Sage screams and she drops the phone so I can't see anything. But damn, do I hear it. It's a melody of curses strung along with pants and moans while she orgasms.

I come soon after, moaning and thrashing my legs around. I try to hold the phone but ultimately drop it on my chest.

"Damn." I pick up my phone, and Sage is back on screen.

"Wow." I smile in my post orgasmic state.

"I know. I need to, uh, wash my hands. I'll be right back."

"Okay." I nod. I should probably wash my hands, too, but I'm too tired.

I push my T-shirt down, prop my phone on the pillow next to me while it's plugged in to charge, and turn on my side. I yawn and close my eyes—just for a second until Sage comes back.

In the morning, I hear light snoring. It shouldn't startle me, but considering I was alone when I went to sleep, it does. My eyes shoot open, and I sit up in bed quickly, looking around the room. I'm about to start panicking, or consider that it was just part of a dream, when I hear it again. My head snaps in the direction of the pillow next to me, and I see the culprit. Sage is still on FaceTime, sleeping in her bed, *snoring*. Has she been on the phone all night? I glance at the clock across the room. It's just after six in the morning. What happened last night? I remember the sexy stuff, and then Sage went to…oh! She went to wash her hands, and I fell asleep. Now that it's all come back to me, I contemplate how to proceed.

"Sage?" I whisper. I hate waking her up, but I don't know what the protocol is.

"Hey." She turns over in bed and smiles at me.

"Hi." I smile back.

"Sorry I stayed on; I just didn't know if I should hang up with you sleeping. I thought you'd wake up, but then I fell asleep," she explains.

"No worries, I was just confused because someone snoring woke me up," I tease.

"I don't snore!"

"Actually, you do."

"Well, damn." Sage frowns.

"Don't worry, it was…cute." I smile.

"Thanks. I should let you go, though, because my alarm will be going off soon, and you do not want to hear that."

"Okay. I'll see you tonight? For ice cream?"

"Yup. Pick you up around seven." She smiles. We both say goodbye and hang up.

I lie back down in bed and smile. I don't think I've ever fallen asleep on the phone with anyone before—let alone woke up and found out they were sleeping right there next to me. It's left a strange feeling in my stomach. Almost like a flutter of hope. I try to ignore it and turn back in the bed to go to sleep. No way am I waking up at six a.m. if I don't have to.

Sage picks me up right on time—,with a bouquet of pink Lillies this time. I smile, already having a vase ready for them in the kitchen. I run back outside and Sage is waiting for me by the passenger side of her car.

"You look cute. I love this romper." She smiles.

"Thank you." I do a little twirl for show, and she laughs. It's light and easy with Sage. Why can't it always be like this?

She hands me her phone when we settle in the car, and I pick the music. This time I choose Halsey's new album. We both sing along to the one song we know and listen to the rest. When we pull up to the ice cream place, we're both deep in discussion about which one of her exes was the worst.

"It's G-Eazy. Like, I love his music, but the man is trash," I say, rolling my eyes.

"Yeah, you're probably right." She nods in agreement.

We wait on the short line and look around, it's fairly crowded, but I spy a table with two chairs, so I tell Sage my order (vegan mint chocolate chip) and make a beeline for them. Five minutes later, Sage is sitting next to me eating her chocolate ice cream in a cup while I'm licking mine off the cone.

"Must you eat it like that?" she mumbles.

"Like wh—" I stop and look at her eyes and the way they look darker than normal. This woman is getting turned on just watching me eat some ice cream.

"Maybe it's just a preview of later." I wink. A bright blush flashes across Sage's cheeks, and I giggle. It's so easy to tease her.

I'm about to make another joke when I look up and I almost drop my cone in my lap. My jaw tightens, and I clench my empty fist. My ex-girlfriend, Jane, and her new girlfriend are standing across the room—and they are feeding each other ice cream…

What the hell are they doing here?

"What's going on?" Sage raises an eyebrow and turns around to look at what I'm looking at.

FOURTEEN

Sage

"That's my ex-girlfriend and the girl she cheated on me with." Heather grinds her teeth.

Without speaking, I move seats from across to next to Heather. I puts my arm around her shoulders and kiss her on the cheek. I don't even know if Jane's looked over here yet, but when she does, I want to make it worth it. I've never seen Heather react like this to someone before. But I understand it.

"Do you want me to do anything else?" I lean in and whisper in Heathers ear. She shakes her head, but just as I think we're in the clear, they start walking toward us.

At first, neither of them notice us. But then Jane stops dead in her tracks just five feet before our table. Heather's too busy eating her ice cream, so I pretend I don't see her. But I can tell it's jarred her to see Heather with someone else. Heather takes a drop of her ice cream, puts it on my nose with her finger and then nibbles it off. It's over the top as far as PDA goes, but from the way they're staring at us, we can tell it's working. I can't help but smile, knowing she's pissed just watching Heather with me.

"Kiss me. Kiss me now," Heather whispers.

I push her hair out of the way to make sure they don't miss this, and I kiss Heather the way I've been dying to all night. Like no one is around us, and it's just for us. Her tongue slips in my mouth, and I can taste the minty ice cream she was just eating. We only kiss for a minute, considering there are families around, but as we pull apart, I see Jane storming out the front door. Her girlfriend trails behind and shoots daggers at Heather on the way out. I can't help but feel quite accomplished.

"Thank you," Heather whispers, looking up at me.

"Anything for my girl," I say with a wink.

We dive back into our ice cream but I can feel the awkwardness between us growing. Jane is just a reminder that all of this is temporary. That what is happening between us is just pretend—a show to make her ex jealous. I knew what it was when I signed up, but I had hoped it might change. Now I'm not so sure that it will.

Heather and I finish our ice cream in silence and then head to the car. She surprises me by taking my hand as we walk to the car. Maybe Jane is still around, and she wants to cover her bases? Either way, I don't mind the way her hand feels in mine. We stop at my car, and I'm about to open her door for her, but instead, she lets go of my hand and places it on my neck.

"Can I kiss you?" she whispers. Her request is different, it doesn't seem like it's for anyone but us.

"Yes." I nod and take a step closer.

She presses her lips to mine, and the taste of mint is back on my tongue. Heather's body is pressed to mine, and I rest my hands on her waist as she puts hers around my neck. This kiss is different, more paced, more purposeful. She's not doing this for show; it's clear she's kissing me because she wants to. I don't know what this means for us or what she's even thinking, but in this moment, I don't care. I let her kiss me for as long as she wants, her hands eventually tangling in my hair and mine slightly grabbing her ass. We don't pull apart until a car beeps at us.

"Are you moving anytime soon? We'd like the spot!" the man yells. His wife makes a face like she's sorry for interrupting us. I notice the kids in the backseat and take a second to compose myself.

"Yup! Right now!" I open the door for Heather, let her slide into her seat, and then I hop in the driver's seat.

We pull out and the family slips into our spot. The moment is slightly ruined but Heather holds my hand while I drive back to her place. She's looking out the window, staring quietly at the night sky. The sun is still up, and I'm thankful for long summer nights. It looks beautiful as the background to Heather.

"Do you want to come in?" Heather asks, chewing on her bottom lip. We're sitting outside her place, and I'm thinking about all the possibilities of what saying yes could mean.

"Yes." I smile. No matter the outcome, I want to spend more time with her.

We walk inside Heather's house, and although I've been here many times now, everything about tonight feels different. I don't know what to say; it's like I've suddenly grown nervous. Heather excuses herself to the bathroom, and I take a seat on the couch. Is tonight the night things finally go further? Are we going to talk about what it meant?

Heather emerges a few minutes later and joins me on the couch. "Want to watch a movie or something?"

"Is movie code for makeout?" I tease.

"It could be..." She looks at me with darkened eyes, and I'm captivated by her.

There's a million things running through my head—so many questions that I could ask. But instead, I pull Heather onto my lap and kiss her. Her lips are fresh with some kind of lip gloss. Is that cherry I taste? Our tongues dance together while her hands begin to roam. Suddenly, my stomach hits me with a weird grumble. Thankfully, she doesn't hear it, so I ignore it. I'm reaching for her ass when it happens again. A second grumble in my stomach, but this time with a sharp pain. I try not to wince, this was probably nothing, and it's not like I want to stop right now.

Heather moans in my mouth, pulling me back into the moment, and I move away from her lips to kiss slowly down her neck. I pepper kisses down her neck as my hands reach for her breasts.

She's grinding on my lap already, and I'm dying to rip her clothes off. But, at the same time, I also want to take my time with her. My stomach grumbles again, but this time a bigger pain hits me, and I noticeably wince.

"Are you okay?" Heather asks, and in response, my stomach grumbles again. Loud enough for her to hear. I'm mortified and freeze.

"Can I use your bathroom?" I excuse myself as she directs me down the hall and to the right.

I lock the door behind me, and I'm thankful for how large the bathroom is. It's not like she could hear me in here from all the way out there. My stomach grumbles again, and I'm sure this isn't going away. I know this feeling. I'm about to kill this bathroom. But what the hell came over me? I was fine when we were getting ice— oh my gosh. I forgot to take my stupid Lactaid pill. I had a huge cup of ice cream, and without that pill, my stupid stomach doesn't know how to digest it. *Great.*

I officially want to die. The last thing I want to do is wreck Heather's bathroom. Especially on the night where it seems like things might go further. But that's done now. No way am I going out there and doing anything but going home. It's not like I could leave now, though. I have to wait for this to pass. Looking around the bathroom, I search for a candle or a window I can open. Then I spot one of those poop sprays, so I spray it a bunch. It won't do much, but maybe it'll help.

I don't know how long I'm in the bathroom, but eventually Heather knocks lightly on the door. I'm frozen in fear, and I can't think of what to say.

"Hey…are you, uh, okay in there?" she asks through the door.

"Yeah. I'm just…" I struggle with what to say.

"Do you need anything?" she asks.

"No!" I shout a little too abruptly.

She doesn't say anything, so I wait and after a minute I call out her name.

"Heather?"

"Yes?"

"Remember how I mentioned I'm lactose intolerant…well, I forgot to take the pill that helps me not have stomach issues when we went for ice cream. So I'm okay, but I might be in here for a bit," I admit. It's better than her thinking god knows what.

"Shit, I'm sorry. I'll go see if we have anything to settle your stomach." I hear her walk away, and I let out everything I've been holding in.

Being lactose intolerant is a fucking joke. Like, it's dairy! Why can't my body just process it normally? Ugh. Heather finally comes back and I tense up again.

"I got some Pepto Bismol here and some Tums. I don't know which works better for you. Do you need me to run to the store and get ginger ale or anything?"

"No, it's okay." She's sweet. I'm in the most embarrassing situation of my life, and she just wants to take care of me. She isn't teasing me or grossed out, she just wants to know I'm okay.

"Okay, I'm going to leave this here and go back in the living room. You call if you need anything else okay?"

"Thank you."

Heather leaves again, and thankfully, it feels like my stomach has stopped attacking me. I take the chance to clean up, wash my hands, and take some Pepto Bismol. It's disgusting, the liquid kind that's the god awful pink color. When I feel steady and sure I'm not going to fart or shit myself, I make my way to the living room.

"Hey, you doing okay?"

"My ego is severely damaged, but the rest of me is fine," I joke.

"Don't worry about that; it happens to the best of us," she says with a shrug.

"Thanks for being so cool about it. But I should get going, I think I just want to be in my own bed tonight."

"Of course. I had a really nice time tonight, before… well you know what I mean," Heather says.

"Before your fake girlfriend almost shit herself on the couch?" I joke.

"Sage!" Heather starts laughing, and it's impossible not to laugh too. I mean, the whole situation is something out of a sitcom.

"I have classes tomorrow and the next day, but then we're still down to go out on Friday right?"

"Yes, I'll text you and we can make a plan." She smiles.

"Nothing with ice cream please," I add for good measure.

"Oh my gosh!" She playfully shoves my shoulder, and I smile. Hey, if you can't laugh at yourself who can you laugh at?

Heather surprises me by leaning in to kiss me goodbye. It's a soft peck on the lips, but still.

"Text me when you get home safe, okay?"

"Sure." I smile.

Slipping on my sneakers, I head out the front door and to my car. As I drive home, I can't help but think about Heather. How much I like her and how much I'm starting to fall for her. Even when I thought I had blown my chances with her, she surprised me. Heather isn't just beautiful and funny, she's kind and thoughtful, and my days are better when I'm with her. I know this feeling all too well, and I should know better than to let her keep being my fake girlfriend. But I'm in too deep at this point. I'm falling head over heels for Heather Owens. But I'm determined to make her my real girlfriend before the summer is over.

FIFTEEN

Heather

"I'm so glad you called, I've been so in my own stuff I forgot you and the girls are only five minutes away again." I smile taking a seat across from Norah.

Her red hair pillows around her delicate face and soft features. We're sitting at the Salty Waves, a seafood cafe in Lovers. It's cute, decked out in fishing nets hanging from the ceiling, and the inside is made to look like the inside of a wooden ship. They don't have too many vegan options, so I don't frequent here, but it's one of Norah's favorite places.

"It's been nice being back in town." She smiles. She had moved back before Alana had asked us to come for the wedding, taking a job at the local bookstore.

"Are you still working at the bookstore?" I ask, sipping my iced tea.

"Yes, they just promoted me to manager actually," she says proudly.

"Wow! Congrats! We should have a drink or something to celebrate," I suggest.

"Oh, I'm actually not drinking right now," Norah says. I don't ask for more, because to me that's enough of an answer. I'm not entitled to know the reason why, even if she says it in an odd tone.

"Dessert later then?" I suggest.

"Sure." She nods. She's quieter than normal, but I don't know if that's just because we haven't seen each other in so long. Maybe we're out of sync.

"How's photography going? I heard you shot that engagement in town last week."

"It's good! Pays my bills and that's what matters. I'm still looking for more permanent gigs but weddings and engagements keep me afloat."

"Here you are." The waiter brings us our food and places the hot plates in front of us. Norah ordered some kind of creamy lobster pasta, and I ordered a portobello mushroom burger with a side of French fries.

We're quiet while we eat a few bites. It's good, not amazing, but I can tell Norah is enjoying herself. I think about telling Norah about Sage, about what's been going on, and asking what I should do. But I don't know if she's ready for that. She lost her husband early last year, and I don't know if she's up for talking about relationships. I know she's not seeing anyone, and I feel like this would be similar. I don't want to bring up anything that might upset her, so I decide to keep Sage to myself.

"So, I kind of want to tell you something." Norah breaks the silence. She wipes her face on the cloth napkin and looks at me with a stoic face.

"What, are you pregnant or something?" I joke to lighten the mood, picking up my glass of water.

"I actually am," Norah says softly and I'm so surprised that the glass slips from my hand, dumping the ice water all over my lap and onto the leather booth.

"Wait, what?" My jaw drops.

"Do you need help?" The waiter runs over with a napkin and a bucket for the broken glass.

"Let's clean up first, then we'll talk." Norah looks at the waiter, and I get it. Lovers is a small town, and she wants to keep this quiet.

"I'm so sorry about this," I tell the waiter before I head to the bathroom to clean up. Ten minutes after standing under the dryer in the ladies room, I give up and call it a day. At least my dress isn't white. It's a thousand degrees out today, so I'm sure it'll dry the moment we step outside.

"Okay." I sit back down and there's no evidence of the mess, except a new cup of ice water in its place. Like I'm going to take a chance on that one.

"Are you okay?" Norah asks.

"Are you?" I'm not just surprised—I'm shocked. "I didn't know you were seeing anyone."

"I'm not." She makes a face. "It's a little complicated."

"Okay… I'm sure I can keep up," I urge her to go on.

"So when Finn passed, we were in the process of attempting IVF. He didn't want anyone to know because he had, well, slow swimmers. He was a proud guy, so he asked that we keep it private. I was actually at the doctor when I got the call that he was in an accident. We stopped the procedure and put the embryos on ice. I figured I'd wait until he was better and we'd try again. But obviously that didn't happen, so I uh, decided recently that I want to be a mom. And I'm not looking to be in a relationship again, so I thought I'd use mine and Finn's embryos and get pregnant. Well, I did IVF and now I'm pregnant, and I probably shouldn't even be telling anyone because it's so soon. I mean I'm just a few weeks along, but I need to tell someone and I know I can trust you." By the end of her confession, Norah is crying. She wipes the tears with the napkin and looks at me for a response.

"Oh my goodness, I'm so happy for you." I stand up and pull her into a hug. I'm probably crushing her but I don't care, one of my best friends is having a baby.

"You are?"

"I would've been happy if it was some one-night stand too, just so you know. I know how long you've wanted to be a mom. I just didn't expect this," I admit as I sit back down.

"I know. I thought about it a lot before I did it. I know it'll be a big undertaking, but I really want to be a mom. And all Finn ever talked about was being a dad. I'd like to give him the chance."

"Of course. And you don't have to worry, I'm sure you and this baby will be okay." I pull her hand into mine and squeeze gently.

"I'm just so worried, I mean, Finn's accident was so random, too. I just worry something might happen to the baby. And then I worry about all the other things attached to being a mom. I'm like a bowl of hormone soup, and I don't know how to process things normally anymore." She cries.

"Hey, it'll be okay. I'm here and I'm sure whenever you decide to tell the girls they'll be there for you too. I mean, you're the one to make us aunts." I smile.

"Well, I'm actually hoping you'll say yes to being the Godmother."

"Oh my gosh!" I squeal, covering my mouth. I'm glad it isn't crowded in here today. "Really?"

"Yes. It's what Finn and I had discussed. He used to badger me to have all these conversations before there was even a baby, and now I'm so grateful he did. I'm going to try to do as many of the things he wanted as possible," she explains.

"I'm sure he's looking down at you two and is so happy just to see you smiling again."

"Yeah?"

"Oh that man would've hung the moon for you. Now to see you with his baby? I'm sure he's ecstatic. I'm just sorry he isn't here to experience it with you."

"Me too." She sighs.

"Dessert menu?" The waiter approaches cautiously. I don't blame him. He's going to be getting a hell of a tip.

"Please bring us one of everything," I say without looking at the menu.

"What?" Norah looks shocked.

"Oh, let's enjoy ourselves." I shrug.

When the desserts come, there's only one vegan option, so I call dibs. I push the rest toward Norah who happily takes a bite of each.

"I'm going to have to unbutton my jeans," she jokes.

"Well, you're eating for two. I want to spoil my godchild as much as I can." I smile.

I pay for everything despite Norah's protests, and I give her a big hug as we leave.

"Call me if you need anything okay? And you tell me when it's not bad luck to buy the kid something."

"Twelve weeks, so you have a bit to go." She laughs.

We say goodbye, and I smile, watching Norah leave. That was the last thing I'd expected to come from lunch, but damn if I'm not ecstatic for my best friend. Instantly, I want to call and tell Sage the good news.

Whoa, what was that? She and I have been spending a lot of time together lately, and I know I'm starting to like her. But am I really wanting to tell her all the little details of my day? I already know the answer, but I'd be lying if I said it doesn't scare me.

I mean, Sage is just my friend. My fake girlfriend. Nothing more, right? Wrong. I don't know who I'm kidding but I know I like Sage ,and I know she likes me back. I mean, who else could wreck my bathroom and still make butterflies appear in my stomach. I don't care what we do or where we go, I just want to be with her. It's scary how easily I'm falling for Sage. I thought I wasn't ready to be with anyone else, but maybe I am. Maybe I could just try.

Pulling into the driveway, I call Sage. We were supposed to hang out later, but I think I want something else. She picks up on the second ring with a happy, hello.

"I was wondering if you wanted to come over tonight?"

"Sure, wanna watch a movie or something?"

"I was actually thinking maybe you could spend the night?"

Sage is quiet for a second, probably taking in what I just asked.

"Like, I should pack a bag and spend the night or like a friendly sleepover?"

"Like you should pack a bag and not expect to get too much sleep," I clarify.

"Oh. Then yes, I would love to." Sage's voice cracks and I laugh.

"I'll make dinner. Something vegan, so don't worry about your stomach," I tease. I know she isn't sensitive about it.

"Ha ha. That sounds good; is eight too late? I'm on my way to the gym."

"Eight sounds great."

"See you then."

We say goodbye, and as I walk into the house, I realize what a mess the place is. I've got two hours before she gets here, and I don't want her walking into this. So, I clean up the empty glasses on the table, throw away the trash, wash the dishes and start preparing for dinner. I set up the ingredients I need and put them in the fridge. I do a quick check of my bedroom and decide to change the sheets. They aren't dirty, but a fresh pair never hurt. I throw everything in the laundry room and make a mental note to deal with that tomorrow. I clean off my nightstand, and then I go take a shower. I washed my hair this morning, so I don't need to do too much, but a quick rinse and touch up down below won't hurt. I find a cute set of matching bra and panties and slip them on under my dress and then run a brush through my hair and redo my makeup. Not too much, since it'll probably just come off later anyway.

Then, I go back to making dinner. I flip through Pinterest, looking for the recipe again and follow the steps perfectly. I'm almost done cooking when I hear Sage's car pulling into the driveway. Suddenly, I feel my stomach doing flips. I take a deep breath and remind myself not to be nervous. This is *Sage*. I feel safe and at home with her. I don't have to worry about her, and I don't need to be anyone but myself with her. She and I are just taking a new step in our relationship, but that's no need for worry. *I* want this. *Sage* wants this. We are two consenting adults, and the thought of sex isn't going to make me sweat through my dress.

SIXTEEN

Sage

I show up to Heather's house with a bouquet of pink hydrangeas and a bottle of wine. Heather and I haven't had more than a glass of wine together, but I thought it fit with what tonight was. When she invited me over to stay, I was nervous. I mean, I'm not an idiot, I knew what she was implying. Then as soon as she opened the door, the nerves dissipated. Heather is standing before me in a light-green sundress covered in flowers. It's something I'm sure I've seen her in before, but somehow she looks even more beautiful in it tonight.

"Come in! You'll let the mosquitos in!" She grabs my arm and pulls me off her front porch.

"These are for you." I smile handing her the flowers and the wine.

"Thank you." She gives me a chaste kiss on the cheek. "I have to check on dinner, but come on in."

She disappears down the hall, and I slide out of my sneakers. Locking the front door behind me, I take a look around. She cleaned up for me; she must be as nervous as I am. I follow the smell of food into the kitchen and she's standing by the stove mixing one of the pots.

"What are you making?"

"Vegan avocado pesto pasta." She smiles and pulls out some bowls from the cabinets.

"Can I do anything?"

"Open the wine? I'll get some glasses."

I pick up the bottle from the counter, and she hands me a bottle opener and places two long-stemmed glasses next to me. I pop the cork and place it on the counter then pour us each a half a glass of wine. Heather pours the food into the bowls and then carries them to the dining room. So I follow behind with the wine. I take a seat and wait while she grabs silverware from the fridge.

"It's my first time making this recipe, so tell me if you hate it," Heather admits.

"I'm sure I won't hate it." I laugh. We both take a bite, and I'm surprised to find I do like it—a lot. I don't want to tell her I've never been a fan of pesto before, but whatever she's doing makes it fantastic.

"So?" she prompts.

"Delicious. Best pesto I've ever had, seriously."

She smiles and I take a sip of the wine.

"How was school today?" she asks.

"Long. I hate summer classes because there's more work in less time. But I don't want to put off graduating anymore," I explain.

"I understand. Did you have any tests this week?"

"Thankfully no, but there was a paper and a presentation due." I sigh.

"Did you do okay on them?"

"I passed both with an A," I say proudly.

"That's awesome."

"Did you have fun with your friend today? What was her name again?" I'm terrible at names. Especially when it comes to Heather's friends; she has too many to keep up with sometimes. I need a cheat sheet to keep up.

"Norah, yes. Actually she had some big news." She twirls her pasta on her fork and looks at me like she's contemplating telling me.

"What was the news?" I ask curiously.

"You have to promise not to tell a soul. I doubt your friends know my friends, but Lovers is a small town, and I don't want to take the chance," she says seriously.

"Of course. Scout's honor." I cross an X over my chest.

"Wait! Were you a scout?!"

"Yeah, I actually was a Girl Scout when I was a kid," I say sheepishly.

"What?! I'm going to need some photos at some point." She squeals.

"Maybe." I roll my eyes. "What was Norah's news?"

"Oh yeah! Well, she's pregnant."

"Wait, isn't Norah your friend who lost her husband?" I ask, not sure if I remember correctly.

"Yes. She decided to do IVF and use their embryos that they already had saved. She only tried once and it worked," Heather says excitedly.

"That's amazing then right? We're happy for her I'm assuming?"

"Yes! And she asked me to be the Godmother," she reveals, proudly.

"Wow." I smile. "Congrats."

"Thanks. I've been like dying to tell you since she told me this morning but I wanted to tell you in person," Heather explains.

"Well I'm excited for her, and for you. Being a Godmother sounds perfect for you."

"I know! I can't wait to spoil the little bean," she gushes.

"Do you like kids?"

"Is that your way of asking me if I want to have kids?" She raises an eyebrow.

I rub the back of my neck. "I was just curious."

"I do want kids, someday. My sister and I are very close, and I've loved the idea of having a big house full of kids. What about you?"

"I like kids. I was an only child, and it was kind of lonely so I always liked the idea of having a few kids when I was older," I admit.

Heather nods and we both ignore the big elephant in the room. We're talking about a future, things that we want when we haven't even admitted aloud how we feel about each other. I decide to not overthink it and tell Heather how I'm feeling.

"I like you, Heather."

"You do?" Heather's wide-eyed, and I can't help but laugh.

"I thought it was obvious."

"I like you too," she says softly.

"I just thought we should say it out loud. Since we've both been kind of dancing around it."

"I don't want to be the first to say it," Heather admits.

"Well, I'm ready to call you my girl if you're okay with that."

"I'd like that." She smiles.

I lean in to kiss her gently on the lips. We finish eating and head to the kitchen. Heather turns on some music while I finish my glass of wine, and she wraps up dinner. I watch her sway around the kitchen effortlessly, she's humming along to the music, but I can't tear my eyes away from her. God, she is beautiful. When she's done cleaning up, she finishes her wine and then walks over to kiss me.

Her hands tangle in my hair while I lean our bodies against the counter, and a moan escapes my lips. She slips her tongue into my mouth, and I run my hands down her sides. I can taste the wine on her tongue and feel her soft hands on the nape of my neck. Her body is humming with sexual energy, and I want to take her on this kitchen counter. But I let her take the lead, I want her to know it's her show and I'm just along for the ride.

"Do you want to move to the couch?" I ask, thinking it might be more comfortable.

"Actually, do you want to move to my room?" She bats her eyelashes, and I swear, if she asked me for a pony right now I'd run out and find her one.

"I'd love to." I nod.

"Okay." She clicks off the kitchen light and holds out her hand for me. I intertwine my fingers in hers, and I feel safe. She brings out this feeling in me that I can't exactly describe, but it's something I've never felt with another partner before.

Her bedroom is huge, with a king-sized bed in the middle that looks freshly made up with light-blue and white sheets. Before I can look around further, Heather pulls me in by the neck for a kiss.

"This is okay right?" she asks, pulling away for a second.

"Yes. And if you ever wanna stop…"

"I know I won't," she whispers.

I take a strand of her hair and brush it behind her ear. She leans her head into my hand and I smile. I could stand like this forever, just looking at her. But there would be time for that. For now, I want to touch my girl the way I've been dying to.

Heather and I kiss, passionately. Our tongues tangle into one, and I suck lightly, causing her to moan. I love getting to know what things she likes. My hands slip over her dress and grab her breasts. They are smaller than my hands, but I don't mind. I can feel her nipples hardening under my touch. Before we both fall into the bed, I pull away from her so I can sit on the edge of the bed. Heather stands between my thighs and flips her hair back. I grab her to kiss her neck, sucking lightly on her collarbone and right under her ear. She gasps, letting me know what she likes.

I go to take off her dress when an idea forms in my head.

"Take it off for me," I command.

"Unzip me?" She twirls around, moves her hair to the side, and I stand. Kissing her from behind, slowly unzipping her dress down to her waist. She slides both straps down achingly slow, and the dress falls to our feet.

Heather's wearing a matching pink lace set. Her panties even smaller than that bikini I saw her in and my mouth waters. Holy hell. How could one woman be so gorgeous? I notice a bouquet of flowers tattooed on her ribs. I'd seen it at the beach but it was prettier up close. Her other tattoos were smaller, and more visible than this. I was going to take my time with her, but seeing her undress for me did me in. I wanted to taste her, and taste her now.

"Lay on the bed for me baby," I instruct and she does. Her legs are hanging off the side as I get on my knees and spread them apart.

Looking up at her pussy, I see a dark, wet spot in the center. "Fuck, is this all for me?"

"Y-yes." She whimpers as I run a finger over the wet spot.

"My girl is soaked, and I've barely touched her," I muse.

Heather waits patiently as I bend forward and run my tongue across the pink lace. Her hips buck involuntarily toward my face, and I chuckle. My girl can't wait to be fucked. I think about making her wait for it, but I'm too eager. I can smell her arousal and the taste through her panties wasn't enough. I want to bask in it.

"Spread your legs," I tell her. She listens and I slide her panties down her legs, tossing them across the room.

I hover over her center, blow a cool breath over her clit, and watch as she squirms for me. Then, before she can protest, I dip my tongue deep into her pussy, running it up the center and all the way toward her sensitive bud. Heather moans, her hips raising, and I hook my arms under her thighs to keep her steady. I kiss her clit softly, learning how much she can handle. Then I flatten my tongue and run it back and forth from her hole to her clit, tasting her completely. She's sweeter than I anticipated, and I wonder if that's because she eats so healthy. I can't get enough. I suck lightly on her clit, and she gasps my name. It only makes me do it again, because I've never heard my name sound so sexy.

"Please! Don't stop!" she calls suddenly, and I realize she's closer than I thought.

I suck just a little harder on her clit, then run my tongue down her center. Over and over again. Soon, Heather is screaming my name. Her hands are in my hair, pulling a little too tight, but I don't let up. Her legs are shaking, and I can feel her pussy pulsing under my tongue. I think I've died and gone to heaven, and if that's true, I'm happy to stay where I am.

"Yes! Oh Sage!" she calls one last time before attempting to push my head out of the way. I kiss her swollen clit one last time, and she gasps for me.

I look up and she's covering her eyes like she has something to be embarrassed about.

"What's wrong baby?" I wipe my mouth on the back of my arm and lie in the bed next to her.

"I didn't know— I'm not usually so *loud*." She's blushing profusely.

"Baby, don't you ever worry about that with me okay? Being loud is more than okay with me." I move her hands from her face and make sure she hears me.

"Okay." She nods. I can tell this might take more convincing, but I would happily make her come over and over if it means she'll continue to be that loud.

SEVENTEEN

Heather

"Come here," I whisper to Sage. I feel completely underdressed, considering she just ate me out, and she's still fully clothed.

So I pull her into me, our lips meeting and our tongues doing all the work. Then I slide my hands under Sage's T-shirt and throw it across the bed. She's wearing this thin, black sports bra, and I can see her hardened nipples through it. Her breasts are smaller than mine, but I still want them in my mouth. So I reach for the bottom of the bra and toss that aside too. I stop kissing her, push her back into the pillows, and climb on top of her. My legs are straddling her thick thighs, and she puts her hands on my waist. I lean down to take one breast in my mouth. Swirling my tongue around her nipple, she begins to moan lightly under me. I let my teeth graze against it softly, and she moans even harder.

I palm the other one with my hand, taking her nipple between my fingers. Then I switch, making sure to give both her breasts attention. Then I slide my hands down her abs and unbuckle her jeans. She gives me a hand with pulling them off and then she's lying in my bed in just a pair of boxers. Fuck, why is it so hot to see a woman in a pair of boxers? Instead of taking them off at first, I slip my hand under the waistband and find her pussy dripping for me.

"Holy fuck. You're wetter than I am," I say, amazed.

"Mmm," she mumbles and squirms against my hand.

I don't want to tease her, so I let her take the boxers off and dive into her pussy. I taste her sweetness and I groan. Fuck, she tastes good. Letting my fingers slide inside her, she lets out a moan. I pump slowly, my fingers sliding in and out easily. Her juices were dripping all over her thighs, too. I kiss the insides of her thighs, nipping a little, and she gasps.

"Fuck," she utters.

I curl my fingers inside her and suck lightly on her clit. But I can tell she wants more. So I add a third finger, and I suck even harder. Which makes Sage squish her thighs against me. With my free hand, I reach to play with her breasts. My hand playing with each nipple until I feel her pussy tightening against me.

"Fuck. I'm coming!" She moans and I don't let up. I keep up with what I'm doing while she perfectly rides out her orgasm. At the last second, she pushes me away and I climb next to her on the pillows. I kiss her lips gently, and she groans as she can taste herself on my lips.

We both lie quietly for a while, until I have to pee. So I excuse myself, and by the time I'm back, she's in her boxers and nothing else.

"I don't like sleeping naked," she explains.

"I don't either." I laugh. I was going to grab a T-shirt from my drawer when I spot Sage's T-shirt on the ground. I pull it over my head and climb into bed next to her.

"I could get used to the sight of you in my shirt." She smirks.

"I could get used to this," I say snuggling into her side.

Sage kisses the top of my head and flips off the bedside light. I think about talking, or asking for round two. But instead, I do a deep yawn and fall asleep soundly.

In the morning, I'm woken up from light snoring. When I glance over and see Sage, I immediately close my eyes and fall back asleep. It feels like hours later when I'm being shaken awake.

"Heather," Sage whispers my name.

I open my eyes and smile, seeing Sage next to me.

"Hi."

"Good morning." She leans in and kisses my lips.

"What time is it?"

"A little after ten." She smiles. "I didn't know if you had any plans today."

"Just this." I smile, pulling her into kiss me again.

"I have morning breath." She groans, pulling away.

"So do I. I don't care."

Sage climbs on top of me, throwing back the covers, and I moan. She's even hotter on top of me. How is that even possible? I'm kissing her neck and running my hands over her bare chest. She closes her eyes and tosses her head back in pleasure. One hand steadies herself on my stomach while she grinds on my lap.

"You look like a natural up there," I comment.

"Mmm, I could get used to this."

"Me too. Might even make me a morning person." I wink.

I'm sliding my hands down Sage's boxers when we hear a phone ring. It wasn't mine so I assume it's Sage's. I pull away, as if to ask if she needs to get it.

"We can ignore it," she says, pulling me back to her lips.

I try to focus on us, but when the call comes in for a third time, I pull away. "Just go get it, or at least put it on silent."

"Okay, I'll be right back. Don't start without me." Sage winks. The sight of her walking through the house topless is one I won't forget.

I sit up in bed, taking the opportunity to check my phone. There are some notifications, but nothing urgent. I take the chance to put my phone on silent. Then I lie back in bed, waiting for Sage to return. The longer she takes, the more I start to worry about her. When she doesn't come back after fifteen minutes, I decide to check on her.

"Okay, okay. I just need you to give me an address." Sage is standing in the middle of the living room, writing something down on a notepad I had left out.

"Sage?" I whisper quietly. She turns around looking distraught.

"Promise me you'll be okay until I get there?" Sage pauses while the other person speaks. "Okay. I'll be there as soon as I can." She hangs up and turns toward me, letting out a deep breath.

"Hey, what's going on?"

"It was my best friend Maeve. She had a fire at her apartment, and her brother...he might not—they're on the way to the hospital." Sage is clearly trying to keep it all together. I can't tell if it's for my sake or hers.

"Okay. What do you need to do?"

"I need to go. Maeve needs me. I need to be there," Sage says.

"Alright." I nod.

Sage walks back toward the bedroom and begins getting dressed in last night's clothes. She picks them up from all over the floor while she paces. I slip out of her shirt and hand it to her. Then, I grab a dress from my closet and a fresh pair of panties. I don't know what to say or how to help with something like this.

"Sage?" I say quietly. Her head whips in my direction, and it's like she knows exactly what I need. She walks over to me and holds me close. She pulls me in for a long hug, I relax into her arms. She kisses the top of my head and then holds my face, looking into my eyes for just a moment.

"I'm sorry, but I have to go. Her brother is her only family. It's complicated with her parents and—"

"Hey, you don't need to explain. Your friend needs you." I nod.

"Yeah." I follow her to the front door and watch as she grabs her things and puts her sneakers back on.

"Do you need anything? I can come if you need me, but I don't want to overstep."

"I appreciate it, but no. She needs me. I'll try to keep you posted." She kisses my forehead and then pauses. Before turning to leave she kisses me hard on the lips. I know she's thinking about so many things at once, and I don't want to give her more to worry about.

"Drive safe," I say and watch as she pulls out.

I close the door behind me and stand against it for a while. I don't know how much time passes because my brain is a rollercoaster of thoughts. I'm wondering about a million different things at once. Realizing my phone is still on silent, I run to the bedroom to grab it and turn the sound on—just in case Sage needs me for anything.

I don't know how I could be of any help. I mean, I don't know Maeve, I barely know Sage. But that doesn't mean I still don't *want* to help. Sighing, I pick up my panties and decide to clean the house. I know I cleaned before Sage came over yesterday, but I suddenly have an urge to do a deep clean. It's something I do when I'm stressed. Keeping my phone in my pocket— yes my dress has pockets—I start in the bedroom.

I make the bed, pick up my clothing from around the room, and then start on the laundry. I wash the dirty sheets I pulled off the bed yesterday. Then, I head to the kitchen to get started on the dishes from last night's dinner. I wash, dry, and put everything away. I stop for a quick bowl of cereal, and then I clean out the fridge. I wipe down the shelves and throw out any old food. Then I take care of the trash and start in the dining room. I wipe down the placemats and the table, then tackle the living room—which is surprisingly clean, considering it's my most active room.

I look for a vacuum cleaner and find one in the closet down the hall near the laundry room. While I'm vacuuming, I can't help but think about Sage. She's on her way to help her friend, but part of me is freaking out about last night. Had we made a mistake and gone too far? I told her how I feel and now I know she feels the same about me. Does that mean we're suddenly girlfriends? It's more than a skip from being my pretend girlfriend.

It's stupid. I've never let anything like sex define me before. It isn't like I need to have that *what are we* talk. I am a strong, independent woman, dammit. But fuck if I'm not also weak in the knees for

Sage. I'm not used to putting this much into being with someone. The last time I did, I got my heart broken by Jane. I know they're different, but Sage running out of here this morning triggered something in me. Like she got what she wanted and now she's going to leave.

I know it's insane, it is Sage after all. But I can't help the way my brain worries. I'm on my third load of laundry for the day when I finally get a text. I drop the wet clothes to the floor and pull out my phone. Only, it isn't Sage who texted me, it was Jane. My hand hovers over the message, unsure of what to do. I mean, what could she possibly have to say to me after this many months? But I'm curious, so I click on the message anyway.

JANE:

> Seeing you the other day made me realize how much I lost. I miss you. Maybe we can get back together. Can we please talk?

It feels like a gut punch to the stomach. She wants to *talk*? She *misses* me? Is she fucking kidding me? There is no way I'm entertaining even a second of this nonsense. It's not like I had suddenly forgotten what she did to me and how she treated me. No. I deserve better than some half-assed text when I'm sure she's still with her new girl. I swipe away from the message and decide to send another text instead.

ME:

> Come by when you're done at Maeve's. Idc if it's late. I'll leave the light on.

SAGE:

> Okay.

I feel a thousand times better. I finish cleaning and go for a quick drive. I want to grab a few things before Sage comes over tonight. I don't know when that would be or what kind of a mood she'd be in, so I'm prepared for anything.

EIGHTEEN

Sage

"Hey, I'm here." I call Maeve when I get to the hospital. I don't know if I'm supposed to check in or wait in the waiting room. She was too upset when she called to give me many details.

"I'm in bed three, tell them you're my girlfriend or my sister—I don't care. Just get back here." She's been crying, I can tell.

I wait on line to talk to someone about seeing Maeve. "Hi, I'm looking for Maeve Conner."

"Are you family?" The lady raises an eyebrow.

"I'm her sister." I smile, knowing I had a better chance of getting in this way.

"I'll need to see some ID," she says, and I hand her my driver's license.

"She's in bed three. Here's your name tag." The lady hands me a sticker and points me through a pair of sliding doors. I look for the sign for bed three, and I find Maeve itching at the IV in her arm.

"Oh my gosh, Maeve!" I run into hug her, and the second I hold her, she sobs into my chest.

"There was a fire, and my brother carried me out but then he collapsed, and I don't know what's wrong because no one is telling me anything," Maeve explains. I let go of her as she wipes her eyes, and I have to admit, she looks rough.

Her blonde hair is covered in black smoke; what is that called? Soot? Her head has a nasty gash on it with dried blood running down her cheek. Maeve's clothes are all ripped and torn, and she smells like an ash tray. I take a seat on the bed and look at her. I'm not sure what to say, so I wait for her to say more.

"I was so stupid. We were playing soccer with some of his friends from high school, and I rolled my ankle. I wasn't even going to play, but Jeremy had insisted. It might be my fault that he's—" She gets all choked up again, and I hand her the box of tissues from the monitor stand.

"That's why he had to carry you? Because of your ankle?"

"Yeah, I tried to run on it but it hurt like a bitch, and I fell. That's how I hit my stupid head. So he insisted on carrying me out. But you know my apartment; I'm on the third floor."

"He's a firefighter, though, right? Isn't that what you once told me?"

"Yes. He is. But he didn't have all his gear, so he could've inhaled smoke or something. I don't know what to do." I grab her hand and squeeze it gently.

"It'll be okay," I assure her. But we both know they are empty words until she gets an update on her brother.

"Can you have someone check on him for me? I don't think they're taking me seriously."

"Okay, well I am your sister after all." I wink.

"Excuse me?" I walk over to the nurse's station. "I'm looking for more information on her—*my*—brother, Jeremy Conner."

"You're family?" This guy raises an eyebrow at me. Like he doesn't believe me.

"Yes." I nod convincingly.

"Follow me." He sighs and I follow him around the corner.

I've never met Maeve's brother, but I've seen photos of him so I know what he looks like. But what I don't expect is to see Maeve's parents standing beside him. Thankfully, the nurse leaves before it's an awkward family reunion. I stand far enough away that I can see them, but not where they notice me. I'm not sure what to do. I can't just walk up to them and introduce myself. I don't know much about Maeve's family but I know her brother is the only one in her family she still spoke to. We've been friends for years, and as open as she is, she never once elaborated on the reason why.

I wait for Jeremy to speak, then at least I can go back to Maeve with good news. But the way their parents are sobbing over him, I can't imagine they have good news. Maybe it's better she hears it from me. I take a few steps forward and they look up.

"Can we help you?" their dad grumbles.

"Maeve was wondering how her brother was doing?" I say, awkwardly.

"You tell her that it's all her fault," her mother says, locking eyes with me.

"What?"

"He's dead," their father chokes out.

"And it's all her fault," their mother adds before pulling the curtain shut on me.

I step back, stunned by the news, and it's like losing my mother all over again. Holding her hands in her last few moments. The months of chemo and the thought of her going into remission—all of it shattered by a cold that developed and escalated. My mom was one of my best friends, and the thought of losing her all over again haunts me. But today isn't about me. I can process those feelings tomorrow. Today, my best friend is only a few beds away waiting for me to give her the worst news of her life. So I swallow and head back to Maeve's bed.

She's getting her head stitched, but she lights up when she sees me. Sitting up straighter in bed, she looks at me expectantly and I try to give my best poker face.

"Is Maeve okay?" I ask the doctor. I'm not asking her; I need to know if she can handle this.

"Yes, the cut is superficial, so it's only a few sutures. Her ankle is sprained so she should keep off it for a few days, but her lungs are clear and there's nothing else we're worried about."

"Could she have a concussion from the fall?" I ask.

"It's possible, but unlikely. We checked and everything seems normal." The doctor smiles and I nod. I wait for her to finish so I can hold Maeve when I tell her.

The second the doctor leaves, Maeve looks at me expectantly.

"So?" she prompts.

"I saw your brother. Maeve, I'm so sorry but he's gone. He died." I know you have to say the words or people don't process it. They told me that when my mom died. You have to say the words.

"What? No." Maeve's shaking her head and trying to jump out of the bed.

"Maeve. I wouldn't lie to you. He's gone."

"That can't be. He was—he was fine. He was carrying me out, and he was just fine. What happened?" She looks to me for some sort of an explanation.

"I don't know. That's the other thing, I think you should know that your parents are here."

"What?" Maeve's eyes bulge from her head.

"They're with Jeremy," I explain.

"Take me there. Please. Get me a wheel chair or some crutches and take me to see my brother. NOW!" she yells. I know if I don't take her, she'll try to get there herself. So I go on the search for someone to help.

"Hi, my um, sister really wants to go see our brother. You know, to say goodbye. Is it possible to get her a wheel chair or some crutches for her ankle?" I add a smile to my request hoping to sweeten the deal.

"Is that Maeve Conner, your sister?" she says looking over something on the computer.

"Yes." I nod.

"I shouldn't tell you this, but your um parents requested that Maeve not be allowed near him. And they are his legal guardians since he's otherwise incapacitated. So there's nothing I can do, I'm sorry." She frowns like she actually is sorry. I thank her anyway and head back to Maeve.

"Why don't I see any crutches?" she snaps. I've never seen her like this, but I know not to take anything she says personally. She's grieving right now.

"Your parents um banned you from going over there," I explain.

"What?" Her anger turns to sadness. "I can't say goodbye to him? To my brother?"

"I'm so sorry, Maeve." I hold her hand.

"I-I want to get out of here. Just get me out of here, please." She starts crying, and I pull her against me. She cries so hard my T-shirt is soaked with tears. But I don't let go. Because I know this isn't even the hardest part of losing someone.

"Sage? Where am I going to live?" she asks suddenly. And I realize not only is her brother gone, but today she lost everything she owns and a place to sleep.

"You're coming to live with me," I say, as if it's obvious. Because to me, it is.

"You live in a one-bedroom."

"And I'll sleep on the couch or we'll get a pull out sofa. Either way, we'll figure it out. I'm not letting my best friend be homeless. Okay?"

"Okay." She nods. "Can we please get out of here now?"

I nod and head off to track down a doctor to let us go. It takes some convincing, but thirty minutes later, I'm rolling Maeve out to the parking lot and into my car. I check my phone for the first time in a while. I had agreed to spend the night at Heather's house earlier but I know I can't anymore. Maeve needs me and I need to be there for my friend. I just hope Heather will understand. The timing is terrible, and I'm sure she must be anxious about last night and what it all means.

ME:

Hey, I'm sorry but Maeve doesn't have a place anymore. It burned down. She's coming to stay with me, and I need to stay with her tonight. I hope you understand.

HEATHER:

Of course I understand. Can I bring you anything? Have you eaten?

I smile. I knew Heather would be understanding. But no, I hadn't had a bite to eat all day. That was the last thing on my mind. And I'm sure it was the last thing on Maeve's mind too.

"Do you want to stop and grab dinner on the way home?" I ask Maeve.

"No. I'm not hungry." She sighs. I'm sure I have some peanut butter and jelly at home to make a sandwich. I quickly text Heather back that I'll be sure to eat, and we don't need anything but thanks.

My house is a half hour drive from Lover's General, so by the time we get there, it's dark outside. I help Maeve into the apartment and she makes a comment about showering in the morning. Which makes sense, because I'm not sure how she could with that ankle. If she needed help it's not like I haven't seen her naked before. Didn't do anything for me, but I could help out a friend. We'd cross that bridge when we get to it.

"Is it okay if I just go to bed?" Maeve asks.

"Yeah, of course. Just let me know if you need anything, okay?"

Maeve nods and I pull her in for a big hug. I don't know what more to say to her, and I feel terrible. On the way home, the fire Marshall had called and confirmed she wasn't coming home tonight. Then he explained that the fire started in the apartment above her, traveled through the stairs, and set hers and the other two apartments in the building on fire. Jeremy wasn't the only casualty, and several others were injured too.

I make a quick sandwich and turn on a movie to fall asleep to. I'm exhausted from the day and I can only imagine what tomorrow might bring. When I know Maeve is asleep, I grab a blanket from the closet and make a bed on the couch. It's not great, but it'll do. I think about Heather and how comfortable her bed is. How comfortable she was to sleep next to and how I can't wait to do it again.

NINETEEN

Heather

"Can you open your front door? I'm outside, I think," I say into the phone. I'd only been to Sage's apartment once, so I'm not exactly sure if I'm outside the right door, but her car is parked outside, so I'm hopeful this is the one.

"What? You're outside?" Sage's sleepy voice is cute as hell, but that can't be the focus right now.

"Yes." I don't explain further and wait a few seconds for her to let me in.

"Hey." I smile when she opens the door. I guess I do have the right place.

"Hey, what's going on?" She rubs her eyes and yawns. It's early, just after eight a.m., but I wanted to get here before they had breakfast.

"I know you said you didn't need anything, but I want to help. So, I brought breakfast for you and Maeve from Teddy's and coffee from Love in a Cup. I hope that's okay," I say holding up the bag of food.

"Oh my goodness, of course it's okay. Come on in, thank you," she whispers, and looking around, I assume it's because Maeve's still sleeping.

I place the food on her kitchen table and hand her an iced coffee.

She smiles and adds some milk from her fridge to the top. Then she motions for me to sit.

"I can go. I really just came to drop the stuff off. I wanted to make sure you guys were eating."

"Can you stay? Just for a little. I kind of missed you," Sage admits.

"I missed you too." I smile.

She leans down to press her lips to my forehead, and I close my eyes, sinking into the kiss. I'm glad I decided to come over.

"How's she doing?" I motion toward her bedroom, where I assume Maeve is sleeping.

"She's doing as expected. She lost her brother, her apartment, and all her things. The fire wrecked the whole building, and she didn't even get to say goodbye to her brother. I just wish I could do more." Sage sighs.

"I'm sure just being here is enough. And you gave her your bed and a place to stay. She just needs to know she has people right now."

"Yeah, you're right. It was hard being alone when my mom died."

"I'm sorry." We'd talked about her mom before, so I know all the details. I'm sure this isn't easy, it's probably bringing up old, unresolved feelings about it.

"I'm gonna take Maeve shopping today to see if we can get her some new clothes and anything she needs."

"Okay, I wish I could offer more. But Maeve's a different size than me right? She wouldn't fit into my clothes?"

"No, and I think she'd feel better owning her own things again."

"I understand." I nod.

"Morning," Maeve says, walking out of the bedroom. I'm shocked at how she looks. There's a darkness in her blonde curls and ashes on her clothes, and she limps out of the bedroom.

"I was just leaving." I stand to go but Maeve stops me.

"You can stay. I'm Maeve. You must be Heather. I've heard a lot about you." She smiles.

"I've heard a lot about you, too."

"Is that breakfast I smell? I'm actually starving," she says, eyeing the bags.

"Yes, I brought pancakes and waffles from Teddy's. I didn't know which you preferred. Oh, and coffee."

"Can I have the waffles? And I'd love a coffee." She takes a seat at the table in between Sage and I.

"I was just telling Heather, I thought we'd go to the store today. Buy you whatever you need."

"You mean rebuy all my personal items again?" Maeve cracks a smile. "I know you're being serious, but I can't even imagine remembering all the things I lost."

"Why don't you think of it like buying all new things? Maybe instead of replacing what you lost," I suggest.

"Maybe." Maeve takes a bite of the waffles.

"Or, I can run out and buy you some clothes, at least. I don't think it's safe to keep sleeping in those." Sage frowns.

"You can get me new clothes, but I'm not throwing these away."

"Okay." Sage shrugs. At least she's getting somewhere with the clothes.

"Do you think you can hang out here while I go out?" Sage looks to me.

"If Maeve doesn't mind hanging out with me, sure." I nod.

"I don't need a babysitter," she grumbles. "But, I wouldn't mind if you were here when Sage is gone."

"Then I'll stay." I smile. I'm glad I came over, at least I can help in some way.

"Text me your sizes, and I'll pick up what I can. Do you need any toiletries or anything else?"

"Yes, please. The basics would be great."

"Okay. I'll also grab some food while I'm out because my fridge doesn't have much," Sage admits. She finishes eating her pancakes and heads to her room to get dressed.

It's awkwardly quiet with Sage gone, but I'm not sure what to say to someone who just lost everything. I feel like it's better to follow her lead. I don't know what topics are on or off the table. I sip my tea while she eats, and then Sage emerges from the room with fresh clothes and a shiny smile.

"I'll see you both later, okay? Text me if you need anything." Sage kisses me quickly on the lips, and I smile. Maeve raises an eyebrow but doesn't say anything.

Maeve finishes breakfast and retreats to the couch, so I follow her. She turns on *Friends* which I'm sure is either her comfort show or her way of making sure she doesn't see anything too triggering. We watch quietly for a while. But then she starts to sob, and I grab a box of tissues for her.

"I'm so sorry," she cries.

"Please do not apologize for grieving. You went through a huge loss yesterday. Feel those feelings."

She cries and at one point, I offer a hug, which she surprisingly takes. I put my arms around her, and she sobs silently into my chest. I rub her back, trying to comfort her the best I can. I'm sure this is awkward for her, too; we're basically strangers. But if I had lost my sister, I knew I'd be just as inconsolable.

"Do you want to talk about it?" I offer.

"I-I just. I didn't even get to say goodbye to him," she cries.

"You didn't?" I know Sage told me, but I play dumb just in case I'm not supposed to know that.

"My parents and I, we don't—we're not on speaking terms. So they banned me from saying goodbye to him. It sucked, because the last memory I have is him collapsing and being pulled into an ambulance," she explains.

"Is there going to be a funeral? Surely we can sneak you onto the guest list."

"I doubt my parents would allow that. I just wanted a chance to say goodbye." More tears fall down her cheeks and a pit grows in my stomach.

"Maybe you can say your goodbye, just not directly to him. I don't know what you believe in, but if he's, you know, up there…

maybe he can hear you, hear this. So you can say goodbye in your own way."

"I don't know what I believe anymore."

"You can give it time. Or maybe when he's buried you can have your own funeral for him. Sage and I would be there, and you can say whatever you need to."

"I like that idea."

"Then that's what we'll do," I suggest.

"Are you and Sage together? Like for real?" she asks suddenly.

"What?" I'm taken aback by the question.

"I know it started off as something pretend, but it looked pretty real this morning."

"I-I—"

"I'm just asking because she likes you. And it's real to her, so please don't break my best friend's heart."

"I like her too. It's real to me, too," I admit.

Maeve nods. She stays in my arms for a while and eventually falls asleep. I pull a blanket over us, and mindlessly watch *Friends*. I wish there was more I could do, but I know sometimes all you can do is be there for someone. It's a few hours later when I hear the door unlock and Sage comes in with several bags full of things.

"Everything okay?" She looks at us confused.

"She's sleeping," I whisper.

"Are you okay?" she asks and I just nod.

Sage takes the time to put away the groceries and then heads into the bedroom with the remaining bags. She got a lot, but I'm not surprised. I'm sure she wanted to do everything she possibly could for her best friend.

Maeve stirs under me and sits up, looking around confused. "Oh shit, I'm sorry. Did I fall asleep on you?"

"Yeah, but don't worry about it." I laugh.

"Sleeping, crying, I guess it's not the worst thing I can do to you." She cracks a smile.

"Hey sleepyhead. Trying to sleep with my girl?" Sage teases.

"You know I can't help myself." Maeve teases back. I see a sliver of the sass Sage warned me about.

"I should probably be going, but I can come back tomorrow with more breakfast if you want?" I look at Sage.

"Breakfast sounds lovely." She smiles. "I'll walk you out."

"Bye, Maeve." I smile.

"Bye, Heather."

Sage walks me to my car and takes my hand. "Thank you for today. I know it's more than you signed up for but I really appreciate it."

"Don't worry about it. I like Maeve, I can see why you're friends."

"Thanks. Hopefully you don't mind her being around. I'm going to let her stay in my apartment until she's back on her feet. I think she's been through enough."

"Of course. Just don't forget about work tomorrow, I don't know how they'd feel about you calling out three days in a row."

"Actually, I took off for the week. But I do have one class tomorrow I can't miss. So maybe you can hang around again? Just until I get back? I have a test and—"

"Don't worry about it. Of course I can." I nod.

"Thank you." She kisses my lips. This time lingering longer than before. I lean into her arms and she envelopes me tightly.

"Get home safe okay?"

"Okay." I smile and head home.

But on my way home, an idea hits me. It's a little crazy, so I decide to make a quick phone call. Alana will tell it to me straight, and I have a feeling she'll be on board either way.

"What's up girlie?" She picks up on the first ring. I'm sure her phone is perpetually in her hand for wedding business.

"I have something to run by you."

"Shoot."

"So I've been seeing someone—"

"Oh my gosh! That's so exciting! What's her name? Tell me everything!" She cheers.

"Well, her name is Sage, and she's really amazing, but that isn't the point of my call." I chuckle.

"Okay, sorry. Go on."

"So we've been seeing each other for most of the summer now, and her best friend Maeve just had a fire at her apartment—"

"The one on Grove Street?"

"Yes. She was one of the apartments there."

"Oh my gosh, is she okay?"

"Well, she lost her brother so she's not great. But physically she just has a sprained ankle."

"Shit. I'm so sorry. Does she need anything? Can I do anything?"

"Well, that's actually why I'm calling. I was thinking about asking her if she wants to live with me, in one of the spare bedrooms at the house. She lost her apartment and she's staying with Sage, but that's a one-bedroom so I don't see how it could work out long-term. But I don't want to ask without checking with you first since it's not my place."

"Of course she can. That's such a good idea! I thought you were trying to move your girlfriend in, which would be a little U-Haul lesbian of you, but this is so sweet."

"No, Sage and I aren't there yet. I don't want to rush anything with her, but I figured this would be like having a roommate. She lost everything, so I don't know how long she'd be staying there. Is that okay?"

"Of course. All the houses got insulated for winter use a few years back, so honestly, if she needs to stay, she can. But really, if she needs anything else we can arrange a clothing drive for her or something."

"I think this is good, but thank you. I'm so glad I asked." I smile. I had a feeling Alana wouldn't say no, but of course I had to double check.

TWENTY

Sage

"I'm sorry, what?" I look at Heather, confused. Did I hear her right?

"I know, but just think about it for a second and you'll realize it's not so crazy," she points out.

She wants Maeve to move in with her. But I give her a chance to think about the logistics of it. I have a one-bedroom, and Heather has this huge house with at least three bedrooms. I don't know how many total, to be honest, and the living room alone is bigger than my whole apartment. But Maeve and Heather barely know each other. Then again, I barely knew Maeve when we became roommates, and now we're best friends. It was a better idea then, let's say, Heather and I moving in together. It would be way too soon for us, and I don't think she'd be ready for that. Hmm, maybe it wasn't so crazy after all.

"Did you talk to Alana about it?"

"Yes. And I explained the situation, so even if I were to find an apartment in the meantime and move out. She said Maeve is welcome to stay as long as she needs." Heather smiles.

"Shit. You really thought of everything, didn't you?"

"I know you're happy to keep your friend, but long-term it just doesn't make sense. I only work one to two days a week, and the rest of the time I'm home. So she wouldn't have to be alone right away, and I have the space. But I didn't want to ask her unless you were okay with it," Heather explains.

"I think it's a great idea; it's really sweet of you," I admit.

"Why don't you ask her then and tell me what she says. That way there's no pressure to say yes in front of me? You know her better than me."

"That's a good idea." It has only been a few days since the fire, and although Maeve seems okay, I'm sure she's far from it. I had convinced her to see the campus counselor this week when she goes to class, so at least there's that. She missed a full week of school, and the school was understanding of the situation. They were willing to let her come back in the fall and finish then, but Maeve was determined to graduate at the end of the summer with me. I think it's her way of getting her mind off things.

"Call me back then okay?"

"Sure." I hang up and head back into the apartment.

Maeve is eating a bowl of cereal at the table. I take a seat next to her and try to gauge her mood.

"Why are you staring at me like that?" She raises an eyebrow.

"Because I have something to ask you."

"Don't you already have a girlfriend?" she teases.

"Oh shush, you'd be lucky to have me." I roll my eyes. "Heather called and has a proposal she wants me to run by you."

"What is it? I'm not being y'all's third no matter how cute she is."

"Oh my god. No." At least she was somewhat back to her normal self.

"Heather has an extra room at her house, well her best friend's house. And she asked if you'd like to be her roommate."

"I can't exactly afford rent right now," she mumbles.

"Heather doesn't even pay rent, it's her best friend's parents' house. But they let family and friends stay all the time. They even said you're welcome to stay until you get back on your feet. So if Heather moves out first, you can still stay," I explain.

"Seriously?" Her eyes light up.

"Yes, and dude it's a beautiful place. Right near the water, huge bedrooms and the living room is bigger than this place."

"Shit."

"You can see it first if you'd like."

"Dude, I'd live anywhere at this point. I'm not in the position to be picky. Are you okay with this?"

"What do you mean?"

"I don't want to impede on your space with your girlfriend."

"Look, some nights I'll come over and hang out with you, and some I'll just hang out with Heather, and sometimes we'll all hang out. My best friend and girl in one place just seems convenient to me." I shrug.

"Then yes, tell Heather thank you. I think this is the first good news I've heard all week," she says. I know she's fine crashing in my bed, but I'm sure the idea of having her own space again lifted a weight off her shoulders. Especially when you add in the fact that it's rent free.

"I'll text Heather, do you want to go over and see it now?"

"Sure." She nods.

I text Heather the good news, and she lets me know Maeve is welcome to move in whenever. We both know she doesn't have a lot of stuff, so it wouldn't take more than ten minutes to pack the car and head over. Maeve agrees and we take all the stuff I bought. When we pull up to Heather's and well, now Maeve's house, she audibly gasps.

"What kind of rich people shit is this? This isn't just a house, it looks like a freaking mansion."

"You know the other houses we passed on the strip up here?"

"Yeah?"

"The family owns them, too."

"Wow. Well, shit. I definitely don't feel bad about not paying them rent then. They clearly don't need it."

"Hi!" Heather greets us outside with a big smile on her face.

She's wearing these cute pair of jean overall shorts and a crop top under.

"Thank you again for this. It really means a lot," Maeve tells Heather.

"Oh, please. We're roomies now, don't worry about a thing." Heather waves her off. "There's two bedrooms down the hall and one next to mine, so I figured I'd let you pick. I didn't know which one you'd want."

"Oh wow. Okay."

"Go ahead. I'll help Sage with your stuff." She smiles and Maeve heads down the hall to look for a room.

"Hi baby." I kiss her lips and she smiles against them. She seems to be in a really good mood today.

"Hi, do you think we could go for a walk along the water later? Just the two of us," Heather asks.

"Sure. Maeve's been okay today, and I think she's getting tired of me insisting she needs someone with her."

"Okay, I went with the blue room down the hall from you. It's truly beautiful." Maeve smiles.

"Let's get this stuff in there then." I carry the bags down the hall and drop them off. Maeve is right, this room is beautiful. Clearly they hired some kind of a decorator when designing this place.

The three of us help Maeve settle in, and then Heather makes us a late lunch and we all hang out in the dining room together.

"Do you have a fire extinguisher?" Maeve asks Heather during lunch.

"There's one in the kitchen by the sink and there's one in the laundry room because of the dryer. And we have all the alarms needed for the place in every room. I double checked, with everything going on," Heather explains.

"Thank you. I'm still a little jumpy when it comes to that stuff."

"It's only been a few days; it's totally normal."

"Is it okay if I go lie down? I think I need to just decompress."

"Sure. We're actually going to take a walk around the lighthouse. We have our phones if you need us," I say.

"Okay." Maeve nods.

"You can rest on the couch if you want, like, make yourself at home. The couch is magnificent for naps." Heather smiles.

Heather and I clean up lunch and head out for the walk. We drive out to the lighthouse parking lot and head for one of the paths. The sun is setting and the waves are slow as we walk, holding hands along the water.

"I wanted to talk to you about something," Heather says quietly.

"Okay." There are suddenly knots in my stomach as I wait for her to continue.

"I like you, and I think I want this to be real. It's very scary to me, so I need you to take things slow with me. But I don't want to pretend to be yours anymore."

I let out the breath I was holding back and smile.

"I feel the same way," I admit. I'm pretty sure I've felt it since the moment I laid eyes on her, but I don't say that.

"So what does this mean?"

"Heather Owens, will you please be my real girlfriend?" I ask, looking at her.

She blushes and nods. So I push a strand of loose hair behind her ear and lean in to kiss her. Our lips meet, and I'm filled with more emotions than I have felt in a long time. I hold her close, and my heart is beating so fast it feels like it's going to escape my chest.

"There's something else I should tell you," she says quietly. Uh oh, that doesn't sound good.

"What?"

"Jane texted me the other night. She told me she missed me and asked me to get back together."

"Oh."

"I deleted the text without replying, but I wanted you to know. Jane and I had too many secrets when we were together, and I don't want to have any with you."

"Thank you for telling me, I don't want us to have secrets either." I smile. I feel relieved; I was worried for nothing.

We walk farther down the path, looking at the water, and we

both sit on a bench at edge of the water. Heather kicks off her sandals to dip her toes in the water. I keep mine on—I hate just getting my feet wet, but I'd watch her kick and splash all day long. She looks happy…lighter. There's been so much chaos this week, and it's nice to know she's been somewhat of my rock.

"What are you smiling about?"

"You. How amazing you are."

"Oh shush." She waves me off, but I pull her close to me, run my hand down her cheek and to the nape of her neck, and then silence her with a kiss.

"Mmm, that's a nice way of shutting me up." She laughs.

"I can think of even nicer ways too." I wink.

"We have a roommate now!" She gasps, as if I said something scandalous.

"So? Just means, someone will have to be quiet." I wiggle my brow as she chews on her bottom lip.

"That might be a challenge for me," she admits.

"Challenge accepted."

I kiss her again, but this time I run my hand down the front of her overalls, unsnapping one side and tossing the strap to the side. Heather moans under me as I palm her breast with my hand. I realize she's not wearing a bra under her shirt. I groan into her mouth. This woman is going to be the death of me. She runs her fingertips down the nape of my neck, and I lean closer into her. Her legs drape over my lap, and I slide my hands up her bare thighs. Thank goodness her overalls are so short. She pulls back from my lips to kiss my neck, sucking gently as I moan, throwing my head back. Her hands slide down my chest, and she paws at my breasts.

"Let's go home," she says breathlessly.

"Only if you can keep quiet." I smirk.

"I'll try my best."

Heather takes my hand, fixing her overalls, and blushes as we walk back to the car. All my thoughts are dirty and of her. I'm honestly thinking about the mechanics of taking her in the backseat.

But ultimately, I slide into the passenger seat and wait until we get back to her place.

As we walk in, Maeve's sleeping soundly on the couch with *Friends* playing in the background. I smile, tossing a blanket over to my friend, and then I follow Heather to the bedroom.

TWENTY-ONE

Heather

I turn on the lap by my side of the bed and then look as Sage shuts the door quietly behind her. Maeve is fast asleep on the couch so we have a chance to do this, but we should be quiet. I unhook my overalls, kick them to the side, and watch as Sage gets undressed too. Her T-shirt lands on the bed, but her shorts are nowhere to be found. She's hot as fuck in her plaid boxers and black sports bra. I slip off my crop top and expose my breasts.

"You do crazy things to my body, baby," Sage whispers and saunters over to me.

"Can we play some music? Or will that just tell Maeve what we're about to do?"

"It might be a little obvious. Let's skip the music tonight," Sage decides.

I nod and shiver when Sage's fingertips connect with my waist. Her hands move cautiously against my body, and then grab my ass pulling me against her. I look up at her, smiling. This time felt different, like we could take our time with each other. Of course I don't want to, but I know there's no rush here.

"Tell me what you want, baby." She pushes away some hair out of my face, and I smile. I love when she does that. It's like she's trying to see me better or something.

"I think I want to sit on your face," I say, biting my bottom lip. It's something I've been thinking about since last time we hooked up.

"Your throne awaits, baby." Sage lies down on the bed, head on the pillows, and points to her cheeks.

I blush and climb into the bed with her. "Maybe you should warm me up first."

Truthfully, I'm already warmed up. I'm kind of nervous to sit on someone's face. I've never done that before, but Sage takes her time with me, kissing my lips. She sucks gently on my tongue, and I hold back the moan I so desperately need to release. Her hands roam my breasts and play with my nipples. Flicking them both with her tongue and pulling softly with her fingers. Her hands travel south, and she groans.

"I think you're more than warmed up," she teases and slides a finger through my folds. I kick my panties off and maneuver to hover over her face.

"Tap my thigh if I'm hurting you or you need air or something," I say, looking down at Sage. She nods but I can tell she's barely listening because I'm all but dripping on her face.

I hold onto the headboard in front of me as Sage wraps her arms around my thighs and pulls my pussy to her face. There is no more hovering. I am full on sitting, and she is licking away. Sage sucks on my clit lightly, then runs her tongue through my folds. I'm chewing hard on my bottom lip so I don't wake Maeve or let her know what we're up to, but that's proving to be harder than anticipated when my girlfriend has a tongue this talented. She's licking me just enough to bring me to the edge, and then she pulls back each time. It's almost as if she's anticipating my release and denying it. She's teasing me, just enough that I don't hate it.

"Fuck Sage." I whimper out when her nose brushes against my clit.

I don't know how the hell she can breathe down there, but her eyes are closed and she looks like she's having the time of her life. I rock my hips, riding her face, and she picks up the pace. Running her tongue back and forth faster. I'm breathing heavy, but I make sure not to moan. Gripping the headboard, I can feel my orgasm coming, and I rock my hips harder. I want to come so fucking bad. I want Sage to make me come all over her face.

"Right there," I whimper out. My thighs are currently blocking her ears, so I doubt she can hear me but she doesn't stop. I'm about to come, and the only thing I think of to do to stifle the sound, is to bite the headboard. Not hard enough where I'll break a tooth, but enough where the sound is muffled.

The rush washes over me, and I collapse into Sage. Falling back into the bed and she pulls me into her arms. I can't open my eyes because everything is soft and my body is racing. I don't know the last time I came that hard. I am in awe of Sage's tongue.

Fluttering my eyes open, I realize Sage is smiling at me. She presses her lips to my forehead and then to my lips. I can taste myself on her lips, which makes me shiver again. Am I turned on by that?

"How's my girl?" she whispers.

"Mmm," I mumble, unable to form real words yet.

"I'll take that as good." She laughs.

I hate that she could do this so easily to my body. But at the same time— *wow*. When I finally compose myself enough to speak, I praise her and her tongue. She laughs and I just smile, because damn, how in the hell did I get so lucky? I mean, Sage is here and this was possible because, what, I stumbled into Lovers Lighthouse one day? To think of the odds of something like that happening, I'm just in awe. A feeling washes over me, one I know, and I'm trying not to panic about feeling it so soon. I am falling in love with Sage.

"Ready for bed?" Sage asks.

"What about you?"

"You don't have to." She shrugs.

"What if I want to?" I say, climbing on top to straddle her.

"Well, then I wouldn't say no." She smirks.

I draw her in for a long kiss, our lips melting into one and our tongues telling each other everything we're too shy to say. I'm about to slip my fingers into her boxers when I pull back and look at her.

"What do you want me to do?" I ask. This is still new, and I want to find out every kink and desire she had.

"Well, I wouldn't mind if I was on my knees and you ate my pussy from behind. Something about that position has always turned me on," she admits with a blush.

"Fuck yeah, bend that ass over." I nod.

"And, if you want to be a little rough with me I'm into that," she adds as she throws off her boxers.

"I am too," I admit.

Sage is on her knees, ass in the air, facing me, and her dripping pussy is on display. I can see her swollen lips, and I'm dying for a taste. All her tattoos are on full display. A back piece I didn't know she had, her rose-covered arms, and her tattooed legs. I want to take a moment to study each one, but she moves, and I'm distracted by the wet sight in front of me. So I dip my head down, dragging my tongue from clit to hole, and I watch as she grips the sheets with both palms. Oh yes, I could get used to this. I run my hand to her clit, rubbing slow circles with one hand. With the other, I palm her ass lightly—just enough to make a light sound. She bucks forward, falling more into the mattress, so I do it again. This time I do it harder, and the same thing happens. I slap Sage's ass a few more times until her cheek is red and bright with my handprint. Who knew something could look this good? Fuck, what I'd do to photograph her like this. Just for my eyes, of course.

Sage moans under me, and I decide to stop teasing her. I move my hand from her clit and replace it with my tongue. Sucking gently, I graze my teeth lightly over it. Her hands are balled in the sheets, turning red from gripping so hard. But I love knowing I'm the one doing this to her. Literally bringing her to her knees.

My tongue trails through her folds again, tasting her sweet juices and soaking up every last drop. Then, I decide to add some fingers, two to start. Darting forward into her pussy, they're easily tightening around me. Is she really this close? I've been tasting her for a while so I decide to add a third finger to her pussy. Her ass bucks into the air, and I can tell she likes it. So I lick her clit and pump my fingers in and out at the same time. I love watching the masterpiece that is my girlfriend unfold in front of me.

She's shaking and thrashing, and her body goes limp as she moans into the sheets. I can tell she wants to be loud, but you can barely hear her make a peep through the sheets she's buried herself in.

"Mmm, I liked that." I slap her ass one last time and she gasps.

"I'm so sensitive," she whimpers.

"Well, let me know when you're ready for round two," I say wiggling my eyebrow.

"What if I use your toy on you? Because my jaw needs a break right now," she admits.

"Mmm, I like that idea." I nod. I reach for my toy in the night-stand while Sage throws her boxers back on and lies on the bed. She turns to face me, and I hand her the toy.

"It is like mine," she admires. "I thought you were just teasing me that day."

"Well, I was. But yeah, I have the older model of yours. But trust me, it gets the job done."

Sage turns it on, letting the vibrator come to life. She watches as it spins in her hand. I clear my throat, and she laughs. Putting it on the lowest setting, she presses it to my clit, and I gasp. I've never had anyone use my own toy on me before, but fuck. I'm already dripping from tasting her. I'm sure after a few flicks of this, I'll be gone.

"Is my girl wet enough for me to put it in?" Sage's eyes are dark with desire, and I nod. I'm always speechless when she calls me her girl, especially in a sentence like that.

"Y-yes," I say when I realize she's waiting for me to answer.

She slides the toy through my folds and then pushes it inside me slowly. Sage flicks the button on to a higher setting, and I moan aloud. Her hand flies to my mouth and covers it instantly. She pumps the toy in and out of me, and I moan quietly into her hand. Something about her hand being there turns me on even more. I can smell my arousal on her hand, and I know she was trying to keep us from getting caught.

"You need to be quiet, or I'll have to stop. Okay?" She stares into my eyes, and I nod.

"That's my girl," she praises, and I can literally feel myself getting wetter.

She flicks the toy up to the highest setting, and I'm instantly seeing stars. My legs tremble, my thighs shake, and I'm moaning into her hand. It's all muffled, but fuck. I practically forget my name by the end of my orgasm. She flicks the toy off and slowly slides it out of me when I still.

"I'll be right back." Sage kisses my forehead and heads out the door. I assume she's on her way to the bathroom, but at this point, I don't care. I'm in heaven—an orgasm induced one.

Five minutes later, Sage comes back, running into the room roaring with laughter, and jumps into the bed.

"Hey! What about being quiet?!" I remind her.

"I just ran into Maeve," she says, choking back laughter.

"What?"

"She was on her way to her room, and she saw me walking back from the bathroom with your toy in my hand. We both started cracking up, and she went to her room. She said she'd be wearing headphone to sleep tonight." Sage laughs.

"Oh no!" I cover my face with my hands. Why do I feel like I've been caught having sex by my parents?

TWENTY-TWO

Sage

"Where's Maeve?" I ask when I get to Heather's one night. Heather is putting a fresh bouquet of flowers I got her into a vase.

"She said some friends were taking her out for a drink. I think some friends from school?"

"Ah, makes sense." I smile. "Is she doing okay?"

"No, she had a particularly rough day today. I think it was the funeral for her brother, so she was upset. But then we watched a movie together and talked a bunch. She's seeing her therapist in the morning, and I encouraged her to get out. I think she's depressed."

"Yeah, I was worried about that."

"She said she'll bring it up to the therapist, so I'm sure she'll work it out but I wanted you to know. I hope tonight lifts her spirits a bit. At least for a little while."

"There was something else I wanted to tell you." I smile.

"Good news, I hope."

"I talked to my boss, and he's happy to add your photos to the site. He's even offering payment because he saw them and was so impressed," I say.

"Really?!" Heather's smile is from ear-to-ear.

"Yup! I'll send you his email and you can send everything directly to him," I explain.

"Wow! Thank you so much." She kisses me softly.

"So, we have the place to ourselves?"

"Yes, but I actually need to go somewhere." She grimaces.

"Can I come?"

"Of course. I just need to go to my parents' house to use the dark-room they have set up there. But don't worry; they're not home. They're visiting my sister in New York for the weekend," she explains. I'm silently relieved. It's not that I don't want to meet her parents, but I would like at least a little time to prepare for that first.

"Okay." I nod.

Heather drives us over to her parents' house, which is cute and quaint. It's a mid-sized yellow house with a bright-red door and a friendly welcome mat.

"Do I get to see your childhood bedroom?" I ask.

"Yes, if you're good." She winks.

Heather gives me a quick tour of the place, and it's cute. I could see her growing up here. It's all very suburban. It seems like the kind of place you'd also see a dog running around. There are family photos all over the place, ranging from all ages and sizes. It's cute to see a gap toothed Heather holding a camera with blonde hair. I always assumed she dyed her hair. I mean, it's pink, but I never knew what color it was naturally. The blonde is cute, but the pink definitely suits her.

"The dark room is down here, but it's kind of small. Do you mind waiting up here and I'll be right back?" she asks.

"Sure." I nod. "I'll just snoop through your childhood home," I tease.

She rolls her eyes and disappears down the basement stairs. I'm looking at the photos on the fridge in the kitchen, and I spot her parents. Heather looks a lot like her mom. I think it's the eyes and her cheekbones. I flutter down the hall and happen upon a door that says *Heather* on the sign. I wonder if her parents have kept things the same since she's moved out.

I get my answer when I open the door, and it's like walking into a time capsule. There are One Direction posters on the walls as well as several lesbian icons of the 2010s. I'm taking it all in when I hear Heather call my name.

"In your room!" I call back.

"What are you doing in here?" She groans.

"Just getting to know teenage you," I tease. "Why didn't you tell me this is why you loved Harry Styles?"

"Oh, whatever. He's like the only guy I've loved." She rolls her eyes.

"We should take some photos in here. I definitely want to remember this."

Heather holds up her camera, pretending to take a photo, but I take it from her, realizing she's always taking the photos and I never have any photos of *her*.

"What are you doing?" she asks, frowning.

"I'm taking some pictures of my girl so she can see what I see." I hold up the camera and try to take some photos, but Heather holds up her hands. She dances around the room, holding up her hands until she falls back into the bed. I take the opportunity to climb on top of her, straddling her and snap a photo.

"Sage!" She groans.

"Come on baby, smile for the camera."

She sticks out her tongue, so I use my free hand to tickle her ribs. She begins laughing hysterically, so I don't stop. She's cracking up, and I manage to snap some photos. I'm sure they came out blurry as hell, but maybe one of them will be good. Finally, Heather manages to get the camera away from me and turns it on me. I strike some silly poses before taking the camera back, putting it on the night-stand and taking the opportunity to kiss her.

My lips are like magnets to hers; whenever we're in the same room, I can't help but want her. She must feel the same because her lips melt into mine. Before things get too heated in her childhood bedroom, we break apart. Heather heads downstairs to check on her photos and comes back up with some supplies.

"I need to leave some overnight to dry, but we can go back home now. Maybe enjoy some alone time since Maeve is out?" she suggests.

"Yeah, I'd love the chance to see how loud you can get." I wink.

Heading back to the house, we both rush inside. Time is of the essence, so we waste none of it running to her bedroom. Heather's lips are on mine in a frenzy and I let out a low moan when she starts unbuttoning my shorts. I'm sliding down the straps of her dress and helping it down her hips. While she's tugging off my T-shirt, I unclasp her bra. Her breasts spill out perfectly into my hands, and her nipples already hard for me.

"Did you get the thing we talked about?" Heather asks quietly.

"Baby, why are you whispering, and why can't you say the word strap-on?" I laugh. She is so cute when she's being shy. This woman has been on my face more than my face wash at this point, and she's still nervous around me.

"I don't know." Her cheeks turn bright-red.

"Yes, I got it. I actually got two because we forgot to talk about size. So you can choose."

"Where are they?" She looks behind me like I'm going to pull it out of my ass or something.

"Baby, I left it in the car. Hold on, I'll be right back."

"Okay." She frowns.

I start to get re-dressed and she groans. "What are you groaning about? I'm not walking outside naked."

"It's not like anyone would see you."

"I'll be right back." I laugh, and then I press my lips to hers for a goodbye kiss. I head to the car and grab the bag from the trunk.

I get back to Heather's room and close the door, just in case Maeve gets home early. It was one thing to catch me with a vibrator in my hand, but it's another to catch me fucking my girlfriend with a strap-on. I do *not* need her to have that sight in her memory.

"Here ya go." I toss the bag on the bed, and Heather riffles through the boxes.

She holds them up and reads over the contents of each box.

They're the same brand, but one is eight inches and one is ten. I have a feeling which one she'll go with, but I want to provide some options. It is my go-to brand, though, because the straps to wear aren't rough or itchy like some of the other brands.

"This one." She tosses me the eight-inch box and puts the other one inside her nightstand.

"Should I put it on now or…" I wasn't sure if I should wait until we were ready to actually use it.

"Put it on now, I wanna see you wearing it." She bats her eyelashes at me, and fuck, I almost melt in the spot.

I take my clothes back off, basically stripping for her and she watches intently. I take the strap out of the box, wipe it off with the intended cleanser and then put it on. It's easy enough to put on and something about it makes me feel hot. Especially with the way Heather is eye-fucking me right now.

Climbing into the bed with her, I get on top. My body is pressed to hers, and I watch as her breathing gets shallow just from the closeness. I kiss her slow, but she's impatient. Her hands are all over my body, grabbing at my breasts with one hand on my ass. I bend my head down to take her breasts in my mouth. Sucking on one nipple, popping it out like a firecracker and then the other. Then I kiss down her stomach and stop just above her pubic bone. I can smell her arousal, her sweetness just begging to be fucked. I run my tongue across her. Sliding it through her pussy, I watch as she moans for me.

"Scream for me, baby. I wanna hear how bad you want me," I tell her.

Dipping my head back to her center, I lick her until she's wet enough. Then I move so my hips are aligned with her core. Glancing up at her, I get her silent approval, and I push inside her. She's so tight, stretching around the base of the strap. Fuck. I can see her juices covering the base. I look at her face while I push in more and more. I'm careful not to hurt her. But damn, Heather can take it. So I slide all the way in and give her a second to adjust. Just as I do, she's moving her hips and pleading with me to move.

"Oh Sage, fuck me hard," she begs.

I thrust my hips forward, and watch as she calls out my name. Her moans are music to my ears. She's soaked and moaning for me as she holds on tight to my arms, and I buck into her over and over. Then I move my arms from her grip and slide one hand around her throat. I squeeze lightly on the sides, and we locks eyes, moaning together.

"You like that, baby? You like when I choke you?"

"Mmm," she whimpers out with a nod, and I squeeze a little tighter.

Is she getting even wetter? I can feel it all over my thighs, mixing with my own arousal and dripping down my legs. I want to see her come for me. I want her to scream for me.

"I want you to come for me baby. And I want you to scream my name. Understand?"

"Mmm." She nods quickly, and I pick up the pace.

I let go of her throat for just a second to slide her leg up on my shoulder. Her head tilts back, and I grip her throat again. I want to see the look on her face when I make her come. She starts rubbing circles across her clit with her hand, and I feel like I'm going to explode with how hot this is.

"Oh yes! Yes! Right there!" Heather screams.

"That's it, baby," I coach her.

"Oh Sage! I'm coming! I'm coming! I'm fucking co—"

Heather collapses under me, a panting mess. I slide out of her, and her juices are literally dripping all over the place. I take off the strap, leaning it on a towel for now, and then I jump back in the bed to cuddle my girl. It's one of my favorite things about after sex. Just holding her in my arms while we talk about life and kiss. She is always speechless after sex, barely able to open her eyelids for a bit. And at nighttime, she usually falls asleep. So, I pull her into my arms, away from the wet spot she made, and kiss her forehead.

"Oh, we're definitely doing that again." Heather smiles as her blue eyes flutter open.

"Oh yeah?" I push her pink curls out of her face.

"Mmm, but for now, just hold me."

I kiss her lips and close my eyes. There's something special about knowing who you'd be waking up next to.

TWENTY-THREE

Heather

I take a magnet and put up the photos from pride on the fridge. Sage, Maeve, and I look so happy all decked out in our rainbow attire. It's the first time I've seen Maeve genuinely smile in weeks. I've already added a few kissing photos of Sage and I to my room, so I don't put one on the fridge. Maeve doesn't need to see that before breakfast every morning. I do add a group photo to the fridge, though. All the girls, plus our partners—some old, some new. It's like we're all finding who we want to be with.

"Hey, do you want to come with me to get our nails done?" I turn to Maeve, who's lounging on the couch and eating popcorn.

She holds up her hand and sighs. "I probably should, shouldn't I?"

"I mean, you only get your master's degree once." I wink.

"Okay, okay. Give me five to change." Maeve walks back to her bedroom, and I sit on the couch. Becoming her roommate meant I got to know her a lot better—and that includes knowing Maeve's five minutes is easily fifteen minutes.

Sage is at work today, so I send her a text letting her know I'm stealing Maeve for the day. She'll answer on break or when she has a spare moment. Maeve is still grieving, but with her therapist, she's been doing better lately. We had our mini memorial for Jeremy last week. I think that really helped her as more than she expected.

Seventeen and a half minutes later, Maeve is changed and ready to go. There's no place in town, so we drive to the next town over. Because Alana's wedding was next weekend, I'm on strict instruction to get dark-blue nails to match the theme of the wedding. I'm getting the gel kind that lasts weeks so I don't have to come back. It's fun arguing with the woman about how short I want my nails. I wish I would've told her the real reason I need short nails so I could see her look at me in shock.

"Ooo, I like that color," I say, looking over at Maeve's pink toes. It's a bright Barbie-pink.

"I figured go for something bold." She shrugs.

"Are you excited about tomorrow?" I ask.

"Not really. It's going to be more obvious that no one from my family is there for me. And it's not like anything changes tomorrow. I could apply for the same jobs today."

"Yeah, but you get to walk across the stage tomorrow," I point out.

"Oh, yes. The infamous stage. I just hope I don't fall on my face. That's the last thing I need now that my ankles all better."

"I'm sure you'll be okay. But maybe stick to flats tomorrow," I tease.

"You said your friends are coming over later right?" she asks, and it reminds me that we're having an impromptu girls' night to celebrate that Kim is finally in town. It's the first chance we've been able to coordinate all our schedules.

"Yeah, we're going to be drinking and playing games, I think. You're more than welcome to join us. I think Sage is coming to sleep over when it's done, even though, I warned her that might be three a.m."

"Maybe I'll kidnap Sage, then. We can go to dinner or something." Maeve smiles.

"That's a good idea."

So far, the roommate arrangement has been working out nicely.

We all got our Maeve, Sage, and Heather times figured out. Our open communication made that easy for us, and the fact that the house was so big didn't hurt.

Maeve and I stop for drinks on the way home from our mani/pedis. She gets her usual extra caramel iced coffee, and I get my usual iced matcha tea. Sage beats us to the house and is sitting in the driveway on the hood of her car next to a bouquet of fresh flowers. I never grow tired of seeing the flowers from her, and I'm glad that isn't something she stopped doing.

"I'm kidnapping you tonight," Maeve tells Sage when we get out of the car.

"Hello to you too." She laughs. Sage places a kiss on my lips and follows us into the house.

"I have my thing with my friends tonight, so your friend is kidnapping you," I explain.

"Ah, sounds good to me." Sage shrugs.

"What time are the girls coming over?" Maeve asks.

"Uh, about an hour? I just have to put together a charcuterie board and put the wine in the fridge." I sit on Sage's lap on the couch and she kisses my cheek.

"Okay, I'll go get ready to go out then while you two be gross." Maeve makes a face and disappears into her room.

"A few minutes with you all to myself? Whatever should we do?" Sage wiggles her eyebrows.

"Oh no, save that for later. We don't have enough time for that."

"I was thinking we could cuddle; what were you thinking?" she jokes, as if she's the innocent one. We'd never leave the bedroom if it was up to her.

"How about some kisses?" I suggest.

"Works for me." She pulls me in and our lips meet.

My hands run through her dark hair as our lips linger. I want to kiss her forever. She's so amazing that it's hard to be apart from her sometimes. I think about tonight, and I want to cancel, ask her to stay instead. But I know it's important, and I want to see my friends. I just also have this urge to see my girlfriend naked too. Not like she doesn't spend most nights in my bed. She still has her apartment, and she goes there to shower and study, but we both like it a lot better when she wakes up in my bed.

"Honey, I'm home!" a voice calls through the room. "Well, look what we have here."

I pull back from Sage to see Ryleigh standing in my doorway with a bottle of Vodka in one hand and a bottle of whiskey in the other.

"Ryleigh!" I jump out of Sage's arms and hug my best friend.

"Who's this hottie?" Ryleigh looks over her sunglasses at Sage.

"This is my girlfriend, Sage," I say proudly.

"Nice to meet you." Sage smiles.

"What are you doing here so early?"

"I thought you might need help setting up. So I brought these and there's a case of chips in the car from the bar," she explains. The bar? I didn't know she had a connection to Teddy's. But then it hits me—she's been staying at the other Lovers estate house with Wrenn. Wrenn worked at Teddy's. I'm just glad they were getting along.

"I can grab them if you'd like?" Sage offers.

"Keys are in my back pocket." Ryleigh turns to show Sage her ass, and I snatch the keys from her back pocket, then smack her ass.

"Hands off," I warn.

"Oh come on. I'm just being friendly." Ryleigh laughs and heads for the kitchen.

I hand Sage the keys and she goes to grab the chips. Maeve finally emerges from her room in a new outfit, and her hair washed, so I take that as a good sign. I introduce her and Ryleigh before she takes off with Sage.

"So what's the deal with you and the hottie?" Ryleigh asks shoveling a handful of chips into her mouth. I'm setting up the charcuterie board that she called 'unnecessary' but she also thought we might play spin the bottle later so I can never really tell where Ryleigh's head is at.

"What do you mean?"

"Why is the Maeve chick living here instead of her? Like, lock that shit down man."

"Maeve is a good friend of ours, and Sage and I aren't ready to live together. We've only been together a few months," I point out.

"If you say so." Ryleigh shrugs.

"What about you? I don't see you bringing anyone special over?" I tease.

"Actually—"

"I let myself in! We were gonna wait but I still have a key!" Alana calls out.

Ryleigh and I rush to the front to help our friends. After our greetings, I grab the snacks they brought along with them. Alana, Ryleigh, Kim, Norah, and I all settle in the living room. Everyone's sipping wine, except Ryleigh who's drinking a whiskey neat, and Norah who's pretending she's having a vodka cranberry, but in reality it's just cranberry juice. I made sure to text her ahead of time and ask what she needed. She isn't ready to tell anyone else yet, which I understand, so I want to make her feel more comfortable. We wouldn't have made an issue if she didn't drink, but it would definitely raise a few eyebrows.

"So are we playing strip poker or what?" Ryleigh asks.

"Or what." Norah laughs.

"Stop trying to get us to take our clothes off." I shake my head.

"Sorry for wanting to celebrate body positivity." She laughs.

"Is everything set for the wedding, Alana?" Kim asks.

"I think so! I just need to make sure I pick up my dress this week. You all picked up yours right?"

"Yes," we say in unison. We got the many, *many* group text reminders.

"I brought Cards Against Humanity, if you want to play that." Alana smiles. She was somewhat of the ringleader of our little group.

We all agree, and she grabs it from her purse by the door. She hands out the cards, and we are all in giggle fits by our third glass of wine. Clearly this game was meant to be played by drunk adults because we're having as much fun playing it as we did when we were fifteen. I pour everyone new drinks, and we start another round.

When the game is finished, we decide playing charades is a good idea. Except half of us don't know how to act shit out, and the other half is too drunk to read the words on the little papers. We're a fit of laughter when Alana tries acting out being an author, and we somehow thought she was being George Washington. I smile, having missed my friends and nights like this—all of us together, just being silly and having a good time.

"Our Uber is hereeee!" Alana calls suddenly.

"There are Ubers in Lovers?!" I ask, shocked. I didn't think it was a big enough town.

"She means Will. He's our designated driver tonight," Norah explains with a smile.

"Ohhhh." I nod.

Alana and the girls run outside to meet Will. Alana and Kim forget their shoes, and Ryleigh forgets her purse. Norah makes sure to grab everything and gets in the car with them. Will laughs when he sees Alana attempting to do a cartwheel across the lawn.

"I can do it! Just let me try!" she yells.

"Come on, get in here." He shakes his head with a smile on his face.

"You'll never catch me!" Alana tells him and runs across the yard away from him.

The rest of us are cracking up at the sight. I mean, Alana is shoeless, drunk off her ass, and running away from her very understanding fiancé like she's a toddler. You can tell that man clearly loves his fiancée. He hauls her drunk ass into the car and buckles her in. Then, he checks on the rest of them and drives away with a wave.

I walk back into the house alone, look at the mess, and decide to leave it for the morning. It isn't going anywhere, and I do not want to deal with it now. Sage and Maeve still aren't back from dinner or wherever they ended up, so I grab my fresh glass of wine, head to my bedroom, and pull out my phone. I have an idea.

TWENTY-FOUR

Sage

I'm still at the bar with Maeve when I get a text from Heather. I almost choke on the beer I'm sipping when I realize it's a naked photo. She's standing in front of her full-length mirror in her room, completely naked. My eyes glaze over the photo as I take in every inch of my magnificent girlfriend. I scroll out of the photo and look at the text she sent with it.

HEATHER:

cum home.

I don't think she's misspelling anything.

"Are you ready to go?" I ask Maeve.

"Sure." She nods. She'd been watching the TV for a bit now anyway.

"Here." I hand her my credit card to pay.

"I'll be right back." She laughs.

Thankfully, Maeve isn't in the mood for drinking tonight, so she offered to be my designated driver for once. I can't remember the last time I went out drinking. I think I had a few beers and maybe a shot or two. Either way, I'm drunk and grateful Maeve is taking us home. I'm sober enough that I can walk straight, and I'm not sick. I'm in that sweet spot of being just drunk enough where everything feels buzzy.

"All paid." Maeve comes back with my credit card, I scribble a signature, and then I write a hearty tip.

Maeve finally got access to her car after not having it from the fire. She lost her only set of keys, and it had taken awhile to get a new driver's license. But now she has everything—and a new set of keys. I think that's partially why she didn't mind driving tonight.

"Come on, let's get you home to your girl."

I let Heather know we're on our way home and she says she'll be waiting in her room for me. Which makes my mouth water. Fuck. I was about to get lucky as hell. Shit, I needed to pee.

"Our house does have a bathroom." Maeve laughs.

"Did I say that last part out loud?" My eyes widen.

"You did," Maeve smiles. She turns into the estate. "Don't worry, I'll be keeping my headphones on tonight I'm sure."

"We aren't that loud." I blush.

"I don't want to risk knowing what my friends sound like in bed." She shakes her head.

"True." I shrug.

We pull into the driveway and she pulls next to my car. The porch light is left on and Maeve unlocks the front door.

"Have a goodnight." She waves me off while heading toward the kitchen.

I race to the bathroom and pee before heading to Heather's bedroom. When I open the door, I find Heather bent over her dresser, her ass completely exposed except for a bright pink string in the middle of her ass cheeks. She stands up straight when she sees me and my eyes almost pop out of my head. She's wearing a lingerie set that's completely see through, with little hearts covering the thin lace her breasts and pussy. It's tied on the bottoms by two small ribbons and looks extremely rip-able. My mouth waters at the thought.

"Hey baby." I walk over to her.

"Hey babe." She chews on her bottom lip. Her eyes are dark with desire and I spot the glass of wine on the nightstand.

"Have you been drinking?" I raise an eyebrow.

"Yes, but I'm not drunk. I really want this." She runs her hands down my chest and pulls me by the belt loops into her.

"Same here." I mumble. I run my hands down her back, down to her ass where I grab ahold of one cheek and grab fiercely.

"Mmm, I want you to fuck me." Heathers lips pull away just far enough to tease me.

She takes my hand, leading me to the bed and I sit down on the edge. Heather walks to the nightstand, pulling out the strap on we bought and places it on the bed next to me. Then starts undressing me. It's slow and she runs her fingertips across my bare skin. Every single nerve ending feels like it wants to explode. My button up is off, my sports bra is across the room and she's tugging off my jeans.

"You're so fucking hot." She kisses my neck, biting harder than normal and I moan. Her teeth graze across my nipples and her tongue circles my belly button.

"Fuck," with the alcohol in my system, every sensation is multiplied by a thousand. It feels so fucking good to just be touched by her.

"Lay back." She commands. I wasn't used to her taking charge with me before, but I do as she says.

Heather slides off my boxers and then gets down on her knees. Which, fuck I have to take a mental picture of. Because my girl on her knees, wearing this skimpy ass lingerie and the look in her eyes? I could cum from this alone. Thankfully I don't. I lean back and watch as Heather's tongue connects with my pussy.

"Oh fuck!" I call out. Heather smiles against me and then slides her tongue up and down my pussy lips. Through the center and glides around the clit.

"Mmm," She hums against my core.

I take a fistful of her pink hair and grab it, pulling her up to look at me. "Fuck me baby," I command and she fucking smirks. I push her back against my clit and her tongue goes wild for me.

She was desperate for every last taste of me and I was desperate for a release. Heather's tongue works its magic around my clit and I grip her hair as my orgasm builds. She's moaning and humming against me, which only fuels me on. I move my hips closer to her face, and she slides two fingers inside me. I fall back into the bed and she continues going.

"Oh my god. Right there!" I gasp. Before long, I'm seeing stars. My pussy contracting around her fingers and I let out a deep moan.

Never had I had a woman on their knees for me like this. Nor had I cum this fast before. But damn, Heather was like no other woman. She wipes off her lips, and looks at me with desire. She climbs onto the bed and I swat at her ass. Slapping the right cheek and she looks back at me with a smirk.

I stand, sliding into the strap on and tell her to get back on her knees. I pull her ass to the edge of the bed and slap it one more time. My handprint left behind on one cheek. Why was it so hot to leave my mark on her?

"Are you wet for me baby?" I ask, already knowing the answer. I can see desire running through her barely there panties and dripping down her thighs. But still, I slide my hand up her thighs, over the panties and then slide a finger inside her. I watch as she moans, pumping in and out slowly for her.

"Mmm," I pull my fingers to my lips and taste her. God, I wanted to have more than a little taste.

So before I fuck her, I pull her panties to the side and stick my face in her wet, hot, pussy. Her sweetness running down my tongue as I lick every drop. God, it should be illegal how good she tasted. I would happily die between her thighs if I could.

"Oh Sage." She moans out for me. Only fueling me on.

"Tell me what you want baby," I tell her.

"I-I want you to fuck me…with the strap on." She utters.

"Okay baby," I kiss her clit and watch as she shivers before positioning myself between her thighs.

My hips line up with hers and I enter slowly. She arches her back, her ass in the air and face in the sheets. Her moans are muffled as I thrust my hips into hers. Her panties are shoved to the side so I pull at the strings and it falls to the mattress under us. Bending down, I take a little nibble of her ass.

"Did you just bite me?" She swings her head around to me.

"Yes." I smack her ass as if to say, and what are you going to do about it?

Her face falls back into the mattress and I hold onto her waist to steady myself against her. Fuck, she was so wet I kept almost slipping out. Making sure I was still inside her, I slide one hand to her clit and smile as she moans for me. I wish I could record that sound and make it her ringtone.

"That's my girl, moan for me baby. Tell me how much you like it when I fuck you." I groan.

"Mmm, I love it." Her hands are twisted in the sheets and she's gasping with each thrust. I'm glad Maeve thought to put her headphones on tonight because neither of us are being quiet.

"Tell me how close you are baby."

"I'm almost there!" She calls out.

"Be a good girl and cum for me, baby. I wanna hear you screaming for me." I whisper in her ear.

Before she can reply, I take my spare hand, reaching under for her hair and grab a handful. I pull her back toward me and she gasps out my name. I rock my hips even faster, one hand on her hair, the other on her hips.

"Touch your clit for me baby. Show me how you cum for me." I instruct. Seeing her hand slide beneath us is fucking hot.

She's touching her clit, and I'm thrusting into her like it's my actual dick because fuck sometimes it feels like it is. I can't explain it, but fuck it's hot as hell. Heather begins cursing and I know she's about to cum.

"Oh right there baby, say my name." I tell her.

"Sage! Fuck me harder!" She screams. So I move even faster, thankful for my thighs that get their weekly workouts at the gym.

"Oh Sage! I'm coming!" She yells out and I don't let up. I thrust into her until she's panting and pushing me away. She falls back into the bed, breathless.

I slide off the strap on, and instead of climbing into bed next to her I dive into her pussy. My tongue connects with her just as she asks what I'm doing.

"Oh Sage!" She whimpers and her hands are in my hair. Tugging and pulling, with each gasp.

Fuck, she tasted so damn good. I lick her core and around her clit, she's dripping all over my face and I'm trying to lap it all up. I just can't get enough of her. I can't take my eyes off her while I taste her. Her eyes are shut and she's holding back moans by biting her bottom lip. But little whimpers and gasps escape with each lick.

"Sage, I don't know if I can…"

But I'm prepared to live down here. I don't care if she comes or not, she's enjoying herself then I'm staying down here. I slip a finger in her pussy and she moans. So I slide in another and she's tugging on my hair even tighter. I smile against her, licking up and down her center. Pumping my fingers to hit her g-spot just so. I'm prepared to do this all night, I just want to see her scream for me.

"Sage! Don't stop!" She screams suddenly. I almost laugh, I wasn't going anywhere. But I keep up, letting my tongue do all the work and she tightens around my fingers.

"Stop!" She screams and I break apart quickly. I'm worried I hurt her or something but she's smiling and whimpering. "It's—I'm too sensitive." She mumbles.

So I kiss her inner thighs, and slip next to her in bed. Taking her in my arms and kiss her forehead. I'm in such a daze that I almost let the words *"I love you"* slip out.

TWENTY-FIVE

Heather

"Are you sure this looks okay?" Sage plays with the bow tie on her neck and frowns.

"You look hot, if Maeve wasn't standing right there I'd make you wear only that while I did naughty things to you." I tell her.

"Thanks for thinking of me." Maeve was next to me in the master bathroom, putting on her makeup.

"Anytime." I wink and giggle. I reach for the curling iron and run it through my hair to get some simple curls today.

"I'm not going to look weird?" Sage frowns.

"Wear what you're comfortable in, but for the record you look beautiful." I kiss her lips and she smiles.

"Okay." She disappears toward my room and I go back to fixing my hair.

Maeve finishes her makeup and heads to her room to get her clothes. She was wearing this really cute pink dress with matching heels. Her blonde curls were looking fabulous and she looked gradu-ation ready. So I put on some makeup and meet Sage in the bedroom. She's standing in front of the mirror, pursing her lips.

"Is it the outfit or the bowtie?" I ask.

"Both? I don't know. I like it, I think I'm just nervous." She sighs.

"Why? Today's the easy part. You just have to walk across a stage, shake a hand and get a paper. You did all the work already."

"That's true." She nods.

"Are you worried about something else?"

"Well, I just know you were looking to move after the summer ends. And now it's basically over."

"I was looking to move somewhere in Lovers. I'm not going anywhere. I mean maybe I'll find an apartment around here and move there, but I'm not suddenly leaving town." I explain.

"Oh, okay." She smiles.

"Come on, we don't want you guys to be late." I take her hand and pull her into me. I hold her for a moment and kiss her lightly.

Sage smiles and we go to the living room where Maeve is waiting for us. We drive over together, me the designated driver for the day. Sage holds my spare hand and I relax a bit. It was a quick drive to the university but finding parking was turning out to be a pain and a half.

"I'll just drop you both off here and find my seat on my own. You texted me my ticket right?" I ask.

"Yes, you're in the middle left."

I kiss Sage goodbye, wish them both luck and watch as they walk off holding their graduation gowns and caps in hand. I drive around the parking lots for what feels like an hour. Glancing at the clock, I had ten minutes to get inside. Groaning, I leave the third parking lot and make way for the last one. It was a further walk than I was willing in heels, but I guess it would have to do. There's one last spot so I grab it, park the car and run toward the auditorium.

My seat is squished between two families but I don't care. It wasn't about me today, I was here to see my girl graduate. So I catch my breath and look around for Maeve and Sage. I finally spot Maeve's big blonde curls in the eighth row and I wonder where Sage was. But she was in cap and gown and her hair blended in with most of the population.

Graduation is long as hell, but when it's Sage's turn I stand up and holler as loud as I can. Everyone's clapping and cheering for everyone so I doubt she can even hear me but I shout anyway. I was a proud girlfriend after all. Then for Maeve, I do the same. I felt bad that there was no one but me here on her behalf today. But I hope she knows that Sage and I would be here regardless of if we had to be.

At the end, I'm one of the first people out the door and I decide to get the car and pull around to meet them. No sense in trying to wait in the crowd. Sage points out my car and pulls Maeve's hand toward it.

"Hi grads, need a ride?" I smile. Sage kisses my lips. Maeve fakes a groan in the background.

"Come on, I thought we'd head somewhere nice for dinner."

I knew a good place that had vegan food, right on the border of Maine. It was a bit of a drive, but it was worth it. Maeve falls asleep in the back seat while Sage and I talk.

"Your present is in the glove box." I point.

"You didn't have to get me anything." Sage says.

"Oh stop it, you're graduating. Of course I did." I wave her off. "Besides, it's something small."

She opens the glove box and pulls out the pink envelope. She raises an eyebrow but is quiet as she opens it. I keep one eye on the road and the other on her reaction.

"Congrats on moving up?" She looks confused. The she opens the card and the key falls into her lap.

"A key?"

"It's to my place." I smile. "I know we're not ready to move in together, but I thought about it and I'd like you to have a key. Which is for the summer house, but I want to give you one to my apartment when I have one too."

"Holy crap, I love you." She says and I almost hit the breaks on the car.

"What?" Thankfully we're at a red light and I can face her fully for a second.

"I—I mean. I was waiting for the right moment to say it, but fuck it. I love you, Heather."

"I love you too." I admit.

"You do? You don't have to say it just because I did."

"Keep reading." I point to the card.

"'A key to my place since you already have the key to my heart. Love, Heather.'" Sage reads aloud.

"You just had to be first." I tease.

"What I'd do to kiss you right now." Sage laughs.

"Well, let's not crash the car." I giggle.

"Yes please." Maeve chimes in from the backseat. "It's about time you two fools finally said something."

"Oh shush, go back to sleeping." Sage rolls her eyes.

"We're here." I announce a few minutes later. The parking lot is crowded so I'm glad I made a reservation for us. I assumed with it being the end of the summer, it might be crowded.

Sage rushes around the side of the car to open the door for me and I slide out. She pulls me against her and our lips collide. Her hands hold my back steady as I collapse into her. Sage's kiss is different, as if feeling all the love she's been holding back. I could kiss her like this forever. But Maeve clears her throat in the background and we pull apart, knowing we'll have time for that later.

"What are you getting?" Sage asks as we look over the menus.

Everything looks and sounds so good, I came here a few times with my parents over the years.

"I'm not sure, but tonight is on me so get whatever you want." I smile. I wanted to treat them both to a nice meal out.

"You don't have—" they both start but I wave them off.

"Just let me treat you both for once, okay? It's your graduation after all."

"Okay." They both groan but then order cocktails so I know they're actually listening to me.

We end up with a round of vegan nachos and some hummus, then a round of drinks while we wait for our meals and we all already had desserts picked out.

"Did you decide where you want to work in the fall?" Sage asks Maeve.

"I was offered a job at the high school doing social work there. I might take it since it's close enough to the house and I can stay in town but I haven't locked anything down yet." Maeve smiles.

"Gotcha." Sage takes a bite of pita and hummus.

"Did you tell the lighthouse you're done doing tours?" I look at Sage.

"Yes, my last day is on Thursday and I'm sort of bummed but they said I'm welcome back anytime. But I'm excited to start my new job." She says proudly. Sage got hired at a family services here in Lovers.

"When do you start the new job?" Maeve asks.

"After the wedding, I asked for a week since I knew there might be a lot going on with Alana's wedding and such." Sage explains.

"Yes, I might need you to help keep the bride sane. She's been under so much pressure lately she's been so stressed."

"When you two get married you should hire a wedding planner so there's no stress." Maeve teases.

Sage and I almost choke on our drinks. Maeve was opening a can of worms we hadn't really talked about yet. We both knew we wanted the same things, but that was also a ways off. Thankfully the waitress comes to clear our food and we're able to sidestep having to make a comment.

"I'm going to force myself to take another bite, because if I don't I'll regret it." Maeve says scooping one last bite of vegan ice cream and chocolate cake onto her spoon. She then pushes the plate toward Sage and I, so we finish it.

"No need for a dairy pill for this ice cream, huh?" I tease Sage. Thinking about that date where she hid out in my bathroom.

"Oh don't start." She groans.

"What are you guys talking about?"

"Nothing!" Sage says a little too loudly.

"Sage had ice cream on a date once and then camped out in my bathroom because she forgot to take her Lactaid pill." I explain. I wouldn't tell anyone else, but this was Maeve. She probably knew worse stories about Sage than I did.

"Oh no." Maeve's mouth hangs open.

"Yes, yes. It was a normal reaction, thankfully I made it in time."

"Do you think you'd still be together if you didn't?" Maeve stifles back laughter.

"I don't like this conversation." Sage groans.

"Oh come on, baby. It's all in good fun. I'd probably still be with her as long as she cleaned up." I laugh.

"Alright, like you two have never done anything embarrassing." Sage glares at both of us and we both go mute. "That's what I thought."

The night ends when Maeve and Sage finish their third round of cocktails and I decide let's not push it with the long drive home. The last thing I wanted was to be cleaning puke off the seats of my car later. Maeve helps me carry Sage in, who's a little bit more of a lightweight then she wants to admit. Placing her on the bed, Maeve says goodnight and heads to her room.

"Ooo are you undressing me tonight?" Sage wiggles her drunken eyebrows while I take off her shoes and pants.

"Don't get any ideas, I'm just helping you get into bed." I shake my head.

But Sage pulls me into the bed next to her and kisses me fiercely. "Mmm." She hums into my mouth.

"I love you, but this isn't happening tonight. Sleep it off and we'll have hot morning sex." I tell her.

"Mmm, that sounds good." She smiles, then seconds later she's snoring in my ear.

I get up to finish taking off her pants, leaving her in boxers and to sneak off her bowtie. That wouldn't be comfortable to sleep in. Then I slide out of my own clothes and get back into bed next to her. I run my fingers through her dark hair and watch as she sleeps soundly.

"I really love you." I whisper. Then I place a silent kiss on her cheek and pull her into my arms for a snuggle.

Epilogue I

Sage

In the morning, my head is killing me. I poke open one eye and look at Heather sleeping soundly next to me. I try to poke open the other eye but the sun is too bright in here. I turn over to get out of bed and that's when I spot the 2 pills on the dresser with a full cup of water. Heather must've known how drunk I was last night and prepared me for the morning. I take the pills, then drink the entire glass of water and sink back into bed. Heather stirs in her sleep and I pull her into my arms.

"Good morning gorgeous." I whisper in her ear.

"Good morning." She says back.

"Sorry about last night, I guess I drank more than I should've."

"Don't worry about it, you were celebrating." Heather turns over to face me.

"Did you have fun?"

"I did, you and Maeve are quite fun when you're drunk." She smiles.

I lean in to kiss her soft, delicate lips. We give hell to morning breath and anything like that, when I slip my tongue in her mouth. I didn't care about anything between Heather and I, I just wanted to be with her. So I kiss her feverishly and slide my hand down her chest, to find she's not wearing anything on top. She loved sleeping naked or in one of my t-shirts so this shouldn't surprise me.

"I love you," I murmur against her lips.

"I love you too," She smiles against me.

Bending down under the covers, I take her breast in my mouth. Suckling on her nipple and playing with the other with my hands. Her nipples harden beneath my touch and I run my teeth gently over each one, enjoying the moans Heather elicits.

"Mmm, that's my girl." I mumble before going further under the blankets and licking my way down her stomach. She shivers from the touch of my tongue.

When I get down to her pretty pussy, she's already wet for me. Either she had quite the sex dream, or my kissing is something to write home about. I'd have to remember to ask her later. Taking a long, languid lick, I taste all of her sweetness on my tongue. Smiling, I hum against her core.

"Oh!" Heather gasps as I place wet kisses on her clit.

I suck gently, wanting to drag this out. I wanted to taste her and live in the joy of her. Running my tongue up and down her folds, I watch as she gets wetter for me. Her juices spilling from her core as I tease her with my tongue. Savoring the sweetness that is my girl.

"Mmm, baby don't tease me." She murmurs from outside of the sheets. It was starting to get hot under here. I flip the covers off me and then resume my position between her thighs.

At least now I could see my girl squirming under me. I slide two fingers inside her tight hole and she whimpers my name. I focus on her clit with my tongue while hooking my fingers inside her. Heather's pink hair is sprayed across the pillows and her head is tossed back as her mouth is agape in pleasure. Flicking my tongue over her clit, she begins to spill over my hand. My fingers almost sliding out of her she's so wet. My face was covered in her juices and so was the bed. Fuck. I loved it when she left behind a mess because of me.

"Oh Sage. Please. Please." She starts to beg. I didn't even realize I was still teasing her. It was so easy to get lost in my girl.

"Mmm." I hum against her core and she bucks her hips higher against my face. I lick my lips against her, then focus on her clit again. With a few quick swipes she'll be coming for me.

"Yes! Right there!" She begins to scream.

I move my fingers faster inside her as she gasps. I know she's trying to stay quiet for Maeve's sake so I don't take offense when she puts the pillow over her face to muffle her moans. Only when she pushes my face out of the way do I finally stop. I don't want to let up, make her cum again. But I know when she's pushing me away it means she's too sensitive.

I wipe my face off and slide into bed next to her. The bed looks like a mess but fuck if my girl didn't cum like a goddess. Her eyes are still closed, her hair a mess around her so I quickly fix it so I can see the rest of her face.

"I love when you do that." She says quietly.

"Fuck you?"

"Make love to me." She whispers.

"Mmm, I do too."

"Give me a second to feel my legs and then get your toy because I wanna make you cum just as hard." She smiles.

"Yes m'am." I turn over to the nightstand drawer and slide out one of my toys. I'd been staying over so much lately, it just made sense to keep it here.

"Mmm," Heather sits up in bed and tosses off the covers, climbs on top of me and straddles my lap. Her lips find mine in a haste and I don't hesitate to kiss her.

Heather's hands are in a hurry to take off my t-shirt and boxers. I'm not wearing a sports bra today so I'm naked in no time under her. My pussy was already dripping from tasting her and the sight of her on top of me just adds to it. I reach for her breasts, taking her nipples in-between my fingers and watch as she chews on her bottom lip. God, I wanted to do that. So I pull her forward and tug gently on her bottom lip with my teeth.

"Oooooh." She groans into my mouth.

"That's my girl." I mutter.

Heather dips her head to my neck, kissing and nibbling along my earlobe down to my collarbone. She spends a little time playing with my nipples and then she takes the toy from next to me, turns it on and slides it between us. Her pussy is directly over mine, so I can feel her juices dripping onto me as the toy vibrates against my clit and her thigh. I don't know exactly what she's going for but I'm not complaining.

"Spread your thighs." Heather says as she slides off me.

I do as I'm told and she clicks up the speed on my toy. Rubbing circles across my clit, I moan lightly. I was as good as gone, but I was trying to hold on. I wanted to enjoy this. Not be some virgin who only lasts ten seconds. Heather then dips the toy down my pussy and slides it inside me. I gasp, surprised by how good it feels. It was a versatile toy, but it was usually only played with on my clit. But Heather was in charge and I wasn't complaining here.

She slides it in and out of me, smiling devilishly while she does. I sit up, resting on the pillows so I can watch her as she plays with it. I think she's going to take it out when she turns up the speed and tells me to flip over.

"I want you on your knees, now."

Again, I do as I'm told. Somehow the toy stays inside, the vibration on high and now I'm even more turned on. Something about this position made me feral. Then Heather moves the toy with one hand and smacks my ass with the other. Just enough to warm me up. Then another slap, this one harder. Oh yes, I was going to leave the bed with her handprint on my ass. She keeps going and I close my eyes, unable to focus on anything but the pleasure.

Soon, I'm calling out her name. Mumbling into the pillows and screaming out in pleasure. She only stops once I collapse on the bed. I can feel my wetness dripping down my thighs and suddenly she's there lapping it all up with her tongue. I whimper and roll over.

"I love you." I smile at Heather.

"I love you too." She kisses me and I can taste the mix of us on her tongue.

Epilogue II

Heather

"I'm sorry you can't come." I tell Sage as I put on the pink dress over my head.

"It's okay, it's your friends and I know it's something small. Just wish Norah luck for me." She smiles.

Ryleigh had reached out to plan a surprise gender reveal for Norah. Now that she'd told all of our friends, she thought we should do something to show our support for her. So she convinced Norah to give her the envelope with the gender in it and she's taking care of the rest. We were told to wear the color we think the baby is and no significant others. Norah was still wrapping her head around all this, so we didn't want to spook her with a big party.

"It's not too much pink?" I frown looking in the mirror. I usually stay away from wearing a pink dress with my pink hair, but I had a strong feeling this baby was a girl.

"I mean, for any other day? Yes. But for this? Nah." She shakes her head.

"I don't know what I'm going to do without you there." I slide my arms around Sage's waist.

"Come on, you'll be fine. It's your friends after all."

"But I'm going to miss you." I bat my eyelashes at her and she groans.

"You know I'd come with you if I could. Just call me when it's over and I'll take you out to dinner."

"There's going to be food there." I point out.

"Food you can eat?"

"True. Okay, dinner with you it is." I smile and kiss her lips softly.

Sage walks me to the door, where Maeve is watching a movie on the couch. I had a feeling this is where Sage was going to be spending her day too. I put on my heels, grab Norah's present, my camera, and give Sage one last longer kiss. Maeve groans in the background and I toss a pillow her way. I know she just likes to tease us about the PDA, and we're definitely not as bad as we could be.

"I'll see you later." Sage waves goodbye and I head out to my car.

It feels weird going somewhere without Sage. It wasn't like we were inseparable, but we had spent a lot of the last few months together. If we wanted to be alone we'd stay at her place, but most of the time we spent it at mine. Maeve was doing better, but we knew she liked it better when we were home. Even if she was wearing her noice cancelling headphones.

Pulling into the estate Norah was staying in only takes three minutes to drive to. It's on Alana's property and looks vaguely similar to my house. Huge, painted a light blue and a swirly driveway around the front. It was near the water, but not as close as mine was to the lighthouse. Norah had been staying here for months, I'm not entirely sure when she got here but I know it was definitely before the summer started. She moved from her big house she had with her husband and needed time to figure out her next move. Of course, now the baby is that next move.

"You made it! Come on, everyone's around the back!" Ryleigh cheers from the front yard. She must've heard my car pulling up.

I slide my sunglasses over my eyes, and balance my camera, my phone and the present in my hands. Thankfully, Ryleigh gets the door for me. I notice that she's not dressed in blue or pink like the invitation said. The invitation that she sent out.

"What's with the black? I thought there was a theme here?" I nod to my overly pink attire.

"Well, I know the gender so I didn't want anyone reading into my dress choice." She explains.

"That's smart."

"Heather!" Everyone greets me at the back door with a hug and a hello. Ryleigh takes the present from me and puts it on a table under the white tent she must've put up.

"How's the baby mama?" I ask, then realize she's not here yet.

"She's on her way. I had Gemma take her out for the morning so we could set up." Alana explains.

"Who's Gemma?" I begin to ask, but we hear the tires of a car out front and everyone rushes around, looking for a place to hide. Apparently Norah knew about the party but didn't know when it would be.

"Why are we going outside? Can't we just go lay down? I'm so ready for a nap—" Norah's voice carries through the kitchen then stops when she sees the decorations.

"Surprise!" We all jump out and she smiles.

"Oh you guys! I said I didn't want anything big." Norah wipes away a stray tear.

"This isn't big, I had to talk Alana down from the 3 tier cake she wanted." Ryleigh teases.

"Hey! Babies are a big deal! I just wanted to spoil the little nugget." Alana smiles. I notice her blue top and white pants, so she must think it's a boy.

"Are you going to introduce me? Or I can go hide out in my room if I'm not invited." The woman next to Gemma teases. She has dark hair like Alana and is wearing a blue sundress that shows off her thick curves.

"Everyone, this is Gemma." Norah smiles. "She's Alana's maid of honor and has been spending the summer here."

Gemma's smile fades but is quickly replaced by a fake smile to say hello to everyone. I silently wonder what was going on there. Why hadn't Norah mentioned her before if they were roommates?

"Before you take a seat mama, you have to pop the balloon and tell us what you're having." Ryleigh instructs. I look around the room, Alana and Gemma were in blue, but Kim and I were in pink. So it was evenly split.

"Okay, I'm so nervous." Norah walks over to the cake table where Ryleigh is untangling a huge black balloon.

Norah looks so cute, she's wearing a soft white sundress but it's just tight enough to show off her bump. It's not much, but if you look you can see the distinct outline. She touches her stomach absentmindedly and then holds the balloon. I turn on my camera quickly so I don't miss anything. I know I didn't need to, but this is a moment Norah wouldn't want to forget.

"Okay, ready?" Norah is handed something small, a pin maybe and she closes her eyes before poking the ballon. Out bursts bright pink confetti all over her and the ground.

"Yes!" I exclaim and everyone laughs. I knew it.

"Oh my goodness!" Norah smiles and Gemma is there to hug her first. Norah wraps her arms around Gemma's neck, and Gemma holds her tightly. As if they hugged often. It felt more intimate than two friends would hug. Was I reading into this?

Everyone takes turns hugging Norah and congratulating her. Then we cut into the cake and all take a seat at the table. Norah at the head, where Gemma waits on her. I almost wonder if I'm seeing things, but then I decide to look back at the photos. Gemma stares at Norah the exact same way Sage looks at me. Poor Gemma. We've all been there with the crush on the straight girl. But then I notice something else, Norah was looking back at her just as lovingly. Maybe something was going on there.

I decide not to ask about it today. Norah knew she could talk to me about anything and if she wanted to, she'd tell me.

"Are you ready for the wedding, Alana?" Ryleigh asks.

"I think so, I hope so." She chuckles nervously. She quickly turns the subject back to Norah and the baby.

"Thank you guys for being here with me. It means a lot to have your support through this pregnancy." Norah smiles.

The party is shorter than I expect, so I text Sage to meet me outside my house. She's standing outside with a fresh bouquet of flowers when I pull up. I smile, she must've noticed that the last batch wasn't doing so well.

"How was the party?" she asks after kissing me.

"Great, she's having a girl." I say proudly.

"Wow you guessed it!"

"I was thinking, what if we just take a walk by the lighthouse tonight instead of dinner."

"You sure?"

"Yeah, I think I just want to be with you and the water." I smile.

"Sounds perfect to me."

I pull out of the driveway, this time with Sage's hand in mine, and I've never felt more safe.

BONUS Epilogue

HEATHER

"I can't even see you in your pretty dress?" Sage groans as I climb out of bed.

"No, I have to get ready with the girls." I explain. Even though she already knows this.

"Alright, but I better get to see you before you walk down the aisle."

"You're only going to smudge my makeup and ruin my hair." I complain.

"So?" Sage laughs.

"I will see you after the reception and that will be good for both of us." I smirk.

"Fine, but then you don't get to see me in my suit." She teases.

"I've already seen you in it, and it on the floor if you recall."

We might've had a really good time when she put her suit on to make sure it fit nicely. And damn, there was nothing hotter than my woman in a suit. She looked like Ruby Rose with her slicked back hair and unbuttoned shirt. She was sexy as hell. Which is how her suit ended up on my bedroom floor and me on my knees.

"Oh yeah," Sage smirks.

"Come shower with me, then I have to go." I hold out a hand for her after tossing on some pajamas, for Maeve's sake.

"Okay." Sage nods, throws on a t-shirt and follows me down the hall.

I turn on the steamy hot water and Sage climbs in first. We take turns cleaning the other and then pull a thick, fluffy towel around our bodies.

"I have to get going, but I'll see you later." I kiss Sage goodbye in the bathroom and head to my room.

I get dressed in my 'before' clothes of shorts and a t-shirt that smells like Sage. Then I grab my bag of essentials and head over to the hotel for the wedding. Maeve and Sage would be meeting us there later. I was thankful when Alana extended an invitation to Maeve, it gave her a reason to get dressed up.

Alana was getting married at the hotel just outside of town. It was pretty ritzy but her family could afford it. When I pull into the back parking lot, I spot the girls cars and head inside. I was right on time but I had a feeling that was going to feel like I was late. Alana had the bridesmaid dresses delivered directly to her house so they'd be here for us. She had also promised hair and makeup would be done by a team of professionals and we were to come as barefaced as possible.

"Don't worry, you're just getting some pre wedding jitters. They'll go away." Wrenn is holding a tissue to Alana when I walk into the suite.

"What's going on?" I whisper.

"Alana's having some second thoughts." Norah whispers back.

"I just know I love him, but how am I supposed to be sure he's the *one*?" Alana cries. One hand has a Kleenex and the other holding onto a long stemmed champagne glass.

"Can you tell her something encouraging? Were you nervous on your wedding day?" I look at Norah for help.

She shakes her head. "I wasn't nervous at all, I was sure about Finn."

We both exchange a worried glance but before we can say anything, the wedding hair and makeup team walks in.

"Ready?" One of the women smile.

I'm whisked into a chair and told to sit still while someone else pours me a glass of champagne. Norah takes a seat next to me, taking down her gorgeous red hair from the bun it's in, it cascades down her shoulders. I want to talk about Alana but she left the suite with Wrenn and Ryleigh.

"Is she going to be okay?" I ask Norah.

"I don't know, I've never seen her this nervous." Gemma adds from Norah's other side. I forgot she was here as Alana's maid of honor.

"Do you think we should get her mom?" Kim asks.

"No, she was just as nervous about this wedding going off without a hitch. I don't know if she can handle it if something goes wrong." Gemma explains.

"Well, I guess all we can do is get ready then." I frown.

I wished there was more I could be doing but it wouldn't help anything if we all made the wedding start late because no one was ready. Alana would pull it together, I've seen her do amazing things in her life. This wedding would be no different.

The hairdresser curls my hair and sprays some hairspray to make the curls stick. I'm told to put on my dress before they do my makeup, so there's no room for smudging. Thankfully, the dress fits perfectly and I feel like a princess in this. Norah's dress shows off her baby bump but when she holds the bouquet, it's hidden perfectly. All the dresses together look great even in the different styles and body types. Alana made us all look amazing.

"Is Sage coming today?" Kim asks.

"Yes! She's bringing Maeve. So hopefully, she'll have someone to talk to during the ceremony." I smile.

"I brought a date, and I'm going to tell her to find Sage. That way she'll know someone out there." Kim explains.

"Go for it, Sage is wearing a suit and Maeve has a dark pink dress." I tell her as Kim shoots off a text.

"Tell us about your date!" Norah gushes.

"She's really cool. We met this summer since I'm staying at the Harbor Inn. She's a writer and we just hit it off."

"Is she from here?" I ask.

"No, she's from New York but she's lived all over. She's looking for a new place to live for a bit but I don't know. It's probably just a summer thing." Kim shrugs. But I can tell there's something there. I don't blame her for acting like it's casual. It's hard when you don't know if something is going to last or not.

Once I'm all made up and done, I check my phone. Just to make sure Sage doesn't need anything. Which, to my surprise I find a text from her.

SAGE:

Which room you in? Gotta give you something.

ME:

Bridal suite. Floor 21

A few minutes later there's a knock at the door. Sage is standing outside the door with a single rose, looking even hotter than before in her suit. God damn, what did I do to deserve this woman?

"Hey, what are you doing here?" I smile, stepping into the hallway.

"I wanted to bring you this. And I wanted to sneak a peek and see how amazing you look." Sage glances over my hair, makeup, and dress. She groans in approval and I blush.

"Thank you." I take the rose from her and smell it.

"You look amazing, I love you." She leans in for a quick kiss.

"I love you too." I smile. I want to kiss her longer, but I don't want to mess up my makeup.

"Well, Maeve's waiting for me. But I can't wait to see you later." She winks and blows me a kiss before heading for the elevator.

"Who's that from?" The girls ask when I walk back inside.

"Sage stopped by to give it to me." I smile and they all say awe in unison.

I place the rose with my things, so I can take it home later. I couldn't wait to get back home with Sage. I knew how lucky I was to be with her, she never stopped making me feel loved and wanted.

Check out Wrenn and Ryleigh's story in *Hate to Love You*!
Preorder Now!

Acknowledgments

Thank you for staying with me when I changed my mind about a hundred times about what I wanted to write this year. Thank you for sticking with me when I finally decided to write this series. I loved writing Sage and Heather's story and I'm SO hype to bring you the stories of the rest of their friends.

Thank you to my besties Michelle and Vicki for keeping me sane and encouraged.

Thank you to the support of my family for believing in me and giving me support when I severely burnt myself out earlier this year. Thank you for reminding me self care is more important than money.

Thank you to everyone who's picked up this book in any shape or form. You readers are what keep me going.

Also by Shannon O'Connor

SEASONS OF SEASIDE SERIES

(each book can be read as a standalone)

Only for the Summer

Only for Convenience

Only for the Holidays

Only to Save You

LIGHTHOUSE LOVERS

Tour of Love

Hate to Love You

To Be Loved

ETERNAL PORT VALLEY SERIES

Unexpected Departure

Unexpected Days

STANDALONES

Electric Love

Butterflies in Paris

All's Fair in Love & Vegas

Fumbling into You

Doll Face

Poolside Love

Eras of Us

Tangled Up In You

THE HOLIDAYS WITH YOU

(each book can be read as a standalone)

I Saw Mommy Kissing the Nanny

Lucky to be Yours

The Only Reason

Ugly Sweater Christmas

POETRY

For Always

Holding on to Nothing

Say it Everyday

Midnights in a Mustang

Five More Minutes

When Lust Was Enough

Isolation

All of Me

Lost Moments

Cosmic

Goodbye Lovers

About the Author

Shannon O'Connor is a twenty something, bisexual, self published author of several poetry books and counting. She released her debut contemporary romance novel, *Electric Love* in 2021. O'Connor is continuously working on new poetry projects, book reviews, and more, while also diving into motherhood. When she's not reading or writing she can be found watching Disney movies with her son where they reside in New York. She is currently a full time mom and full time author.
She sometimes writes as S O'Connor for MF romances and as Shannon Renee for Poly romances.

Heat. Heart. & HEA's.

Check out more work & updates on:
Facebook Group: https://www.facebook.com/groups/shanssquad

Website: https://shanoconnor.com